THE
BLACK CAIRN

THE
BLACK CAIRN

by

Vena Holm

© 1994
Published by Highland Press

ISBN 0 9524728 0 5

Printed by
Highland Printers, Inverness

Limited edition of 1000 copies

Front cover illustration: Mixed media painting by Sue Jane Taylor.
Inside illustration: Drawing by Rosemary Davidson Taylor.

To Sue and Rosemary, my nieces, without whose help and advice the book would not have been published.

CHAPTER ONE

The day ought to have been different, since he had been longing for it to come as long as he could remember, but it wasn't. Everyone, Colin decided crossly, was determined to make it like any other day. The same old porridge and milk for breakfast, the same old rush to be ready in time, the same old warnings from his mother to remember to do this and not to forget to do that. Then there was Allan, cool and superior as usual, answering all his excited questions with damping matter-of-factness, just as if it was an ordinary day and he was setting off to the village school, as he had done hundreds of times in the last six years, instead of going for the first time with his brother to the Academy seven miles away.

"Now, you're sure you haven't forgotten anything, Col?" said his mother. She had said it at least a dozen times in the last ten minutes, so he did not bother to answer.

"Mind you look after him now, Allan, and see that he doesn't fall out of the train."

"Ah'm no' a baby, ah'm twelve — ah can look after myself," Colin muttered, tugging at the straps of his schoolbag.

"Aye, but you sometimes behave like one," said his mother tartly. "And don't you go wandering off by yourself and getting lost."

"It's Blairinver ah'm going to, no' to London."

At last they were ready and racing down the path that

led to the main road, Allan as usual in front, shouting to Colin to hurry up, that he could see the smoke of the train. On this day of all days, Colin reflected bitterly, he might have waited instead of rushing on ahead to show him that he could run faster. But Allan was waiting for him at the end of the path. Colin's resentment left him at once and he walked along proudly beside his brother, trying to match his long, confident stride.

Perhaps, after all, he had been wrong to want Allan to treat this as a special occasion, to say something that would show that he accepted him as an equal at last. It wasn't in Allan's nature to make a fuss. He ought to be content that he had waited for him, and that showed, just as clearly as words, that he was in Allan's world. Now that he had achieved his ambition, it would be more in keeping with his new status to appear indifferent. Allan's voice broke through his thoughts and, to his dismay, it was not the tone that he had expected. In a flash he realised why he had waited for him.

"There is just something that ah want to make plain to you, Col," he was saying, "so that you won't be getting any ideas into your head. Ah don't want to be telling you in front of all the others, so ah'll just be putting it straight now, once and for all. Ah'm no' having you tagging along behind me. Ye'll have to make your own friends just as ah had to make mine. Are ye hearing me?"

Colin nodded. He was very near to tears, and only by biting his lip and keeping his head down as if he were concentrating hard on his shiny new shoes, was he able to conceal the hurt that his brother's words had caused him. Allan looked at him sideways for a moment, then he went on less harshly,

"That's fine then, so long as ye mind on it. Anyway, ye'll soon get into the way o' things and have your own

2

friends. Come on then, or we'll be losing the train."

He broke into a run and Colin let him go. He did not care now if he missed the train. It would serve Allan right if he did. For a moment he thought of turning back. Allan would catch it if he did. He stood still, his shoulders hunched, his hands thrust deep in the pockets of his new blazer, brooding over the thought of his revenge. Far ahead he could see Allan, who had now been joined by his friends. They were talking and laughing, happy and secure in their world. And he was as usual left out, tagging along behind with never a hope of catching up.

All his life it had been the same. There had never been a time when he had not wanted to be like Allan and to be with Allan. He remembered, for instance, that Allan had said when your age reached double figures, then you were no longer a child. And so, when his tenth birthday approached, he was sure that Allan would accept him as an equal and he would go bird-nesting and fishing with him and his friends. He could still hear the scorn in Allan's voice as he said on the morning of his birthday,

"Come to the Gullies' Moss with us? Are ye daft? It's far too dangerous for little boys. Ye have to be twelve before you can go there, so there's no use ye're thinking on it."

So now that he was twelve, he supposed, he would say you had to be fourteen, or sixteen, or whatever age it was he happened to be himself. He would never catch up with him. He had been a fool to think that because this was to be his first day at the Academy, Allan would be different.

He heard a shout and saw his brother waving to him. He forgot his intention of paying Allan back by missing the train and automatically began to run. He reached the platform as the little engine drew in with a hissing of steam. He followed his brother into the train and along the corridor. His spirits were rising in spite of himself. To

3

be travelling by train, to be an Academy boy, to have a new blazer with a badge, a new schoolbag and a new pencil-case and a magic box of mathematical instruments, to be about to learn at firsthand the things Allan talked so easily of — algebra and geometry and science and Latin, there was more than enough in this to make him forget his disappointment. He threw his satchel into the rack with as good an imitation as he could of his brother's casual gesture, then sat down in a corner seat and listened eagerly to the conversation of Allan and his friends. That in itself was excitement beyond what he had minutes ago hoped for, when he had been standing unhappily in the road wondering whether to go back home. It was characteristic of him that his mood was now swinging to the opposite extreme, for Colin knew nothing of half-measures.

The train shunted into the siding to pick up some wagons and moved off again with a jerk that threw his satchel on to the floor. The conversation stopped suddenly and Allan said, staring at the bag and then at Colin,

"How did you get in here? Don't you know that this is a third year compartment? Your place is down the corridor with the first year."

"Let him be, just for the first day," said one of the others, "he's no' doing any harm."

"That's no' the point. Ah told him he wasna' to be running after me and that's all there is to it. Besides, we have to keep a seat for Jeff."

"Well, let him stay till Jeff gets on."

But even that Allan, with his sense of the right order of things, would not concede.

"It's best he should begin the way he has to go on. Away wi' you now, Col, and mind on what ah told you?"

Red with humiliation, he caught up his satchel and

4

tugged open the sliding door. Out in the corridor he slammed it shut again, with such force that Allan shouted angrily after him. Colin made a derisive face at him and leant his back against the window. It was all so unfair and such a dismal beginning to what he had thought was going to be the most wonderful day in his life.

He stood looking out of the window for a while. The train was shunting back again to pick up the guard's van that had been left behind on the main line. As it went slowly by he caught a glimpse into the yellow signal box where the porter stood with his hands on the levers. This distracted his attention from his grievances. He had always been drawn by the mysterious little shed but never before, because it was kept locked, had he succeeded in getting a proper look inside it. He watched in fascination while the porter threw back the levers, extracting the shiny black tablet, put it into its leather bag and held it out to the driver of the engine, who caught it neatly as the train rolled past. Then the porter ran along the line towards the guard's van. There was a bump as buffer met buffer, and a jangle as he coupled train to van. Then with a jerk they were chugging past the loading bank, where he could see a cart loaded with bags of corn being backed on to the weighing machine. He leaned out and waved to the man who was holding the horse's head and coaxing it into position. Now the train was running through the station and under the bridge, sending clouds of smoke into his face because he had forgotten to close up the window in time.

The little engine was gathering speed now, bravely throwing back cornfields, woods, and telegraph poles, slamming into and out of bridges, running down the hill and coming to a halt with a grinding of brakes and a shudder that ran from engine right through the train to

5

the guard's van. A few passengers got in, including Jeff, who passed him with a friendly "Aye, aye, Col," and thrust his way past him into the compartment. The door clicked behind him, and through the glass he saw him take the place he had vacated and become part of the group. He watched them for a moment, then catching Allan's eye which said as plainly as words, 'Stop glowering at us and find your own place,' he moved slowly down the corridor until he was opposite a carriage where there were five boys, who looked as new as he. They must have got in further down the line for they were all unknown to him. He stood studying them for a moment. The atmosphere was very different from Allan's compartment. There was little conversation and none of the friendly, noisy banter that he had just witnessed. They looked subdued and too self-conscious to take notice of him; all but one, who sat in the corner nearest him and smiled up at him as he came in. He pushed his bag under the seat and sat down opposite him.

Remembering Allan's injunction to find his own friends, he began to study his companions. None showed any sign of wanting to talk to him and he was too shy to make any overtures to them. Only the boy in the corner appeared interested in him. Whenever he looked in his direction, the other's eyes glinted at him and Colin sensed that he was more than willing to talk. Only his first impression was anything but favourable. The boy's head was too large, his face was pale and heavy, and he wore thick glasses which magnified his little black eyes. His body, he noticed with distaste, was fat, bursting out of clothes that were too tight for him, and his legs were too short, they dangled a few inches from the floor. He wished he would not keep staring at him, he reminded him of the picture of a troll in an old story book. To escape his scrutiny, he got up and went to the window.

They were slowing down again, approaching the second station on the branch line. He pulled at the strap awkwardly, for he was not sure how to open the window, then with force that produced no result. Exasperated because he knew that they were now all watching his incompetent efforts, he tugged it with all his strength. It broke off and he was left standing staring foolishly at the length of brown leather. He went back to his seat with the strap still in his hand.

The fat boy leaned over and said,

"Shove it under the seat. They check the tickets here and you'll be in trouble if they see it. Give it here."

He handed it over, too confused and humiliated to say a word. The fat boy thrust it out of sight under the seat with a conspiratorial wink and a nod, which Colin ignored. He was not at all grateful for the help, nor was he pleased when, a few minutes later, he could not find his season ticket and the fat boy suggested looking in the front pocket of his school-bag, and grinned triumphantly when it actually turned out to be there. He was, Colin decided, too smart and too forward, a show-off and to be avoided.

CHAPTER TWO

Thus, when they changed from the branch to the main-line train, he hurried on ahead and found an empty compartment in the hope of shaking him off. The move was unsuccessful. In a few minutes, he saw him peering into the compartment and, oblivious of Colin's cold stare, he seated himself in the opposite corner.

"Ye'll be a new boy," he began.

"Aye," said Colin reluctantly, and having delivered the monosyllable looked pointedly out of the window.

"If you like I could help you, show you where to go and that kind of thing."

"How can you?" Colin answered bluntly. "Ye're new yourself, aren't you?"

"I'm in the first year like yerself, but I'm a Pi."

"Ah don't know what you mean?"

"πr^2, you know. Pi is a repeater and so am I."

"You mean you've been kept back."

"If you want to put it crudely, yes."

"Why can't you say things plainly then, instead of gabbling on about pies?"

"Just ma little joke. When you get to know me better, you'll find I'm fond of ma little joke."

Colin was quite sure he had no intention of getting to know him better.

"Oh, ah didna find it very funny."

"I'll have to do better then, won't I? What's your nomen, by the way?"

"Ah don't know what you mean."

8

"Nomen — the Latin for name."

"Why couldn't you say so, then? It's Colin Fraser."

"Mine's Hugh Rennie, very much at your service." At this, he got up, swept off an imaginary hat and made a low bow.

Colin stared in amazement. The contrast between the fat, awkward figure and the formality was ludicrous. Never in all his experience had he come across anyone so odd.

"What did you do that for?"

"Just a little ceremony. I like to do things in style. Now, I feel that we are properly introduced."

Colin did not know what to make of him. Apart from his comical appearance and strange way of behaving, there was his speech. One moment he was talking in what he took to be a Southern Scottish accent, the next with an English accent. It bewildered him and made him feel at a disadvantage.

"You don't come from here. You talk funny."

"The answer to the former is yes, as to the latter I do not agree. It may sound funny to you, but that, I suggest, is because you've never been out of here yourself. As for me, I have been around a bit. Ah was born in Aberdeen, ye ken, oh aye, in the granite city itsel'. But then, I've spent a few years in Sussex, so you see, I'm a bit of a mixture."

"Aye, ye're that all right."

"Well, they say that mongrels are best." He broke off suddenly, jumped up, pulled down the window and leant out.

They were running along beside the firth parallel to the peninsula where they lived which was served by the branch train they had just left. The fat boy turned to him and said excitedly,

9

"Tak' a look at the Black Cairn, will ye, Colin? There's a heron on't. Aye, an' a shag too. An' there's a shellduck in by the shore."

Despite his resolve not to be drawn, Colin could not resist joining him at the window. Birds were a subject that never failed to interest him.

"There's some redshanks there, to the right of the duck," he said, "and a lot of dunlins too."

"Aye, there's always plenty o' them. And lots o' curlew stalking aboot on the shore."

They had found a subject they were both enthusiastic about and for the rest of the journey they talked of the nests they had found that summer, each trying to outdo the other in bird lore. By the time they reached their destination, Colin, though he was still unwilling to commit himself, was disposed to view his new acquaintance more favourably. Had it not been for the disapproving look which Allan cast at his companion, when they were passing through the barrier, he would have forgotten that his first impression of Hugh had been unprepossessing.

In any case, even if he attempted now to get rid of him, short of being very rude, it was impossible. Hugh was trotting along by his side on his absurdly short legs, talking incessantly. Whatever his feelings, the fat boy was evidently determined to stick by him and Colin had to admit that he was an amusing companion. In fact, he found himself becoming so interested in Hugh's talk about the school and the masters that he did not notice that they were lagging far behind the others. Now and again, Hugh would stop and give an imitation of a teacher or a boy, that Colin could not help laughing at. He was an excellent mimic and had a seemingly endless repertoire. Normally Colin would have disliked being made conspicuous by such performances but, in this case, he was too enthralled to think of that. From humans Hugh passed to bird calls. Here Colin had something to contribute too, and to his delight, the fat boy praised his imitations.

By this time, all the others had long since disappeared, but when Colin remarked on this, Hugh was not in the least concerned. They had reached the High Street and he now turned his attention to the shop windows. Colin, who seldom saw a shop except the tiny one in the village, was soon equally fascinated by bookshops, toyshops, and confectioners, and when Hugh announced that he had a whole sixpence, he willingly entered into the discussion as to the best way to spend it. In the end they decided on a comic, which Hugh promised to lend him when he had finished with it. With the remainder they bought toffee and, chewing companionably and discussing the merits of the stories in the comic, they loitered down the street.

CHAPTER THREE

It was only when they turned into the school road and he noticed it was empty, that Colin realised that they were going to be late. At the same moment, he caught sight of the town hall clock — half-past nine! He was flabbergasted. Half-an-hour late on his first day! Hugh, interrupted in the middle of an account of his last school, was a little put out at the abrupt interruption of his eloquence.

"Ach, ye dinna need to fash yourself aboot the time. It's the first day and they're no' all that fussy about punctuality on the first day. Now, as I was telling you —"

But Colin did not wait to hear any more. He was racing down the road at full speed, turning a deaf ear to Hugh, who on his short legs was completely outclassed, and who was wasting his breath pleading with his friend to wait for him. When Colin reached the school-gate and turned into the playground, he found it deserted, and since he had no idea where to go, he was obliged to wait until Hugh came panting up. The minutes gave him time to reflect that he had been rather mean to rush away, especially with the toffee still in his mouth, and this thought was swiftly followed by another less creditable one — that it was Hugh's fault that he was late.

His resentment, however, quickly turned to contrition when Hugh joined him, gasping and wheezing and quite unable to speak. His struggle for breath alarmed Colin. He stood by helplessly, knowing that he ought to get help, but uncertain where to look for it.

"Wait here, I'll get someone," he said, but Hugh held him back. In a minute or two, his colour became more normal, his breathing easier and he managed to say,

"It's only my old asthma. It catches me like that sometimes when I do anything strenuous."

"Ah'm sorry ah made you run," said Colin.

"Ach, think nothing of it. I'm all right now. Anyway, it's a gran' excuse. I had one o' my turns and you stayed with me till I recovered. How's that?"

"Well," said Colin doubtfully, "ah don't know. It's no' true — no' quite true, that is."

"Leave it to me, Colin. Anyway, I don't think you could put it over very well. You have the kind o' face that gives you away."

Not very sure whether to be flattered or annoyed, Colin followed his new friend into the building.

CHAPTER FOUR

Hugh was right. His story was accepted by the master without question and the two boys were given seats side by side at a double desk at the back of the room. Colin was not at all sure that he wanted to be paired off with Hugh, particularly since the latter insisted on whispering to him comments on the lesson, which was a history one, and imitating the master's mannerisms when his back was turned. History was a subject in which he was very interested and the constant asides from Hugh irritated him, until he felt he could endure it no longer. The worst of it was that Hugh appeared to be completely impervious to his frowns. Finally, to his relief the master noticed the fat boy's clowning and removed him to a desk by himself. Soon Colin was absorbed in the lesson and forgot all about his new friend.

It was a confusing day. No sooner had he become interested in one class than he was whirled away to the next. New classrooms, new teachers, new books and new neighbours — for he succeeded for the rest of the day in avoiding sharing a desk with Hugh — everything was enthralling to Colin's naïve eyes. New languages with weird sounds called phonetics, and poetry, not the dull stuff he had learned at the village school, but real exciting things like ballads that you could get a grip on and thrill to as if you had been there yourself. Most entrancing of all was the thing called science. The room itself was a delight

14

to him, the coloured bottles and the balances with the tiny weights, the retorts, the beakers, the pipettes and, above all, the bunsen burners at either end of the long tables. It was like a miracle to him — electricity or gas had not reached his village yet — when the master turned on the tap, held a match to the end and the thing burst into a lovely blue flame, that hissed and twisted like a snake's head. He couldn't understand why Allan had said the smell of gas that hung around the room made him feel sick. To him it merely enhanced the magic and he was sorry when the bell rang and he had to move on to mathematics. But even this he found, to his surprise, for he was not very fond of figures, was interesting. Geometry, he decided, was very promising and algebra an improvement on arithmetic.

The day ended with a period in the gymnasium. Colin had never seen a place like it in his life. He learned now what Allan meant when he talked about parallel bars and climbing the ropes and jumping over the horse. In the latter he was a little disappointed, for he had visualised it more like a real horse, though, of course, he knew that it was made of wood, but he soon forgot that in the sheer joy of running and leaping and climbing. He even earned a word of praise for his agility. That was a surprise. Hitherto he had had to measure his skill in running and climbing against Allan and his friends, on the rare occasions when they condescended to include him in their ploys. Now he found that he could hold his own with any in the class. To finish up they had a game of handball and there, too, he distinguished himself. All in all, his first day had more than lived up to his expectations and not even the fact that Hugh was waiting for him at the gate — he was excused gym because of his asthma — could take the gilt off it.

15

CHAPTER FIVE

A week went by like a flash, days that were packed with interest and new experiences. He was beginning to get the hang of things, to know his way around the buildings that had at first bewildered him. The fact that he found the new subjects easy gave him confidence and his ability in the gym and on the games field were a source of pride. He was establishing a world of his own and no longer felt the need to look to Allan for his standards. Consequently, he was happier than he had ever been, for he was free of the frustrating feeling of being in a situation where he was destined to be for ever a poor second.

There was, however, one thing which troubled him. Although he was on good terms with most of his school-fellows, he had not yet succeeded in making a real friend. This was partly because he did not find it easy to take the first steps, probably because he had been so often rebuffed by Allan and his friends that he feared to commit himself, and partly because in the first days Hugh clung to him like a shadow and defeated all his attempts to shake him off. No hints appeared to have any lasting effect on him and a kind of loyalty mixed with pity prevented Colin from telling him brutally that he did not want his company.

Besides, there were moments when he could not help being touched by Hugh's devotion and his generosity. There was nothing that the fat boy was not prepared to

16

share with him. He pressed sweets and comics on him and asked for nothing in return, but to be with him. He went to endless trouble to entertain him, and moreover, Colin had to admit that without his help he would not have found his feet so quickly. If only he had not been so odd-looking, if only Allan was not so contemptuous of him, if only it were not so obvious that the other boys despised him, if only he did not stick to him all the time like a burr, and turn his hurt spaniel's eyes on him when he lost patience with him as he frequently did.

Not the least irksome aspect of the relationship was that there were so many things that he would have liked to do, but could not because of Hugh. Anything strenuous brought on his asthma and yet he made pathetic efforts to run and jump and climb trees in order to please his friend. These attacks were so alarming to Colin that he tried to curb his instinctive desire to scale any likely-looking tree, to race along the banks of the canal, to climb walls and fences that might be too difficult for his companion. Naturally, he did not always succeed in imposing on himself such restraint and felt both guilty and resentful when inevitably Hugh tried to emulate him and, in consequence, sometimes brought on one of his fits.

One day, when Hugh had to stay behind after four to finish an experiment, he went off on his own, feeling a slight twinge of conscience at the desertion, but at heart relieved that for once he would be free of him.

There were two ways of reaching the station. One led through the town and was interesting because of the shops. The other, which was the one the boys generally took after school, was longer and followed the bank of the canal, crossed the railway-line and led past the ruins of the old castle, then down an avenue lined with chestnut trees into the station square. It was the one Colin preferred because of the canal, which was dirty and stinking when the tide was out, but there were rats living in the holes in the banks, voles and toads, and fish in the pools, and when the tide was in you could sail sticks or paper boats down it. Presently he came on a group of the train boys. They were absorbed in a game of trying to see who could hit a tin can half embedded in the mud near the far bank. His coming made even numbers, so they decided to have two teams and Colin, happy to have been accepted, was soon heart and soul in the game.

CHAPTER SIX

When that was over, someone suggested they should look for conkers, another that they should explore the castle ruins where, he said, there was a secret passage that led to the Black Cairn in the firth and had been used centuries ago as an escape route by the besieged, when the Norsemen attacked the castle. While they were arguing the merits of the ploys, Hugh came up, pushed his way into the centre of the group and into the discussion. When he heard about the secret passage, he said scornfully that there was no such thing, that he had been there plenty of times last year and there was nothing to see but a lot of tumbled stones and part of the arch of the gateway.

"All the new kids," he said, "go poking around there. Every year it's the same. I'd advise you to save yourself the trouble, you'll only be disappointed. Now, I have a much better idea."

But no-one wanted to hear his idea. His patronising air annoyed them. They began to poke fun at him, mimicking his accent and his appearance, until the fat boy was aroused to fury and turned on his baiters. A fight might have developed in which Colin would have been forced unwillingly to side with Hugh, but at that moment they saw another group of their class-mates coming along the path. They were five boys from the West Coast of the county. Now, between East and West there was a kind of feud. This Colin had often heard about from Allan, and so

19

he was very curious about the boys from the West. He had watched the little group in his own class and decided that, despite the feud, there was one boy he would have liked to know. He knew that his name was Uisdean and that was curious, he thought, because it was the Gaelic for Hugh.

Once or twice, when they had passed and their eyes had met, Uisdean had smiled, but so far Colin had never plucked up courage to speak to him. If he had ever met him alone it might have been different, but he was always with the other West Coast boys. Colin had heard them talking together in Gaelic and that fascinated him. It was true that in a way it put a barrier between them, but at the same time, it made Uisdean even more interesting.

When Uisdean and his friends had passed the group of East Coast boys, Hugh, who was anxious to make the others forget that he had just been the butt of their mockery, began to give a loud imitation of Uisdean speaking English. Colin's attempts to shut him up only had the effect of making him raise his voice to a shout. The West Coast boys stopped, Uisdean said a few words in Gaelic and then the five turned and came back. Hugh edged into the middle of the group from the safety of which he continued his performance.

"We would just like to be having a word with your friend," said Uisdean, in his soft, slow voice.

Though none of the East Coast boys would have cared if Hugh got the beating he deserved, honour demanded that they should defend him. So they closed round him and prepared to do battle.

At first both sides were good-natured. It was more like a game than a fight, with Hugh the prize for the winning side. There was much shouting, shoving and scuffling, but mainly in fun, until Hugh sneaked up from behind

Uisdean and dealt him a vicious blow between the shoulders. At once the good-humour vanished and they began to use their fists in earnest. Colin found himself face to face with Uisdean, with Hugh sheltering behind him, and against his will was forced to defend him. The two boys closed, Uisdean exerting his superior height and weight to throw Colin. Hugh, snatching his opportunity, seized Uisdean by the legs and brought him to the ground. Then before Colin could prevent him he began pummelling and kicking his fallen enemy.

This cowardly attack was too much for Colin. Without realising that he had changed sides, he seized the fat boy by the scruff of the neck and dragged him away. Then Uisdean was on his feet, dazed by the sudden attack but still full of fight. Hugh was not taking any chances. By the time his adversery had recovered, he was off down the canal banks, his short legs covering the ground with a speed that amazed Colin. Uisdean raced after him and soon it was obvious that Hugh was flagging and that it was only a matter of seconds before retribution overtook him.

By unspoken consent hostilities between the others were suspended and everyone watched the race, cheering and shouting advice. They were running very close to the water now and Colin realised that Hugh was making for a tree whose branches, growing close to the ground, he could climb and so hold his adversary off. The question was whether he would reach it in time, for it was obvious that he had little strength left. Colin did not know whether he wanted him to be caught or not. He was still disgusted with him for his craven behaviour but, at the same time, he was so obviously the underdog now and besides, he could not help wondering whether his unaccustomed activity might not bring on an attack of his

21

asthma. And then, of course, he could not quite forget that, despite his mean act, he was an East Coaster and so entitled to his support. When he had changed sides a few moments before, he had acted instinctively. Now, though there was no animosity between the two groups, the old rivalry was still there and Hugh represented the East, however poor a representative he might be. Thus, on the surface at least, he cheered him on like the other East Coasters.

Then suddenly he saw Uisdean stumble and throw out his hands to regain his balance. Next second he had disappeared over the edge of the bank. Again, he acted instinctively. Before any of the others realised what had happened, he was running towards the canal. Seconds later he had reached it and was about to climb down the steep, muddy bank, when he heard a shout. Uisdean, covered with slime from head to foot, was just picking himself up from the mud.

Colin did not quite know whether to be glad or sorry that Uisdean was in no need of rescuing. At the back of his mind, while he was running to his aid, he had had a picture of himself as the hero of the situation, quite forgetting that, in fact, there never had been any danger since it was low tide. Now, he felt awkward and stupid and did not know what to say. Then he saw that Uisdean was grinning and that impressed him. Colin himself, if he had found himself in such a situation, would have been too concerned with the thought that he was looking a fool to see the humour in it. He grinned back at his former enemy and said,

"Ah'll give you a hand up."

"Indeed, I could be doing with it, Colin. It is just a little bit slippery here."

The others had now come up and amid the laughter and

the attempts to give Uisdean a clean-up, everyone forgot the original cause of the fight. When they had scraped some of the mud off and Uisdean had said laughingly that he was sure that mud baths were very good for the health, and that it would be a fine idea to give Hugh a taste of the same medicine, they realised there was no sign of the fat boy. Then someone noticed the smoke of their train in the distance and the East Coast boys raced off at top speed, followed by the encouraging shouts of their late adversaries. They reached the station, stormed over the bridge and piled into the corridor just in time. Exhilarated by the adventure, they were much too busy reliving it to notice that there was still no sign of Hugh. However, when they reached the junction and changed into the little branch train, he joined them looking a little subdued and uncertain of his reception. Since they were in high spirits, they tolerated his presence, and only when he began to boast of how he had worsted Uisdean did they tell him bluntly what they thought of his sorry part in the affair. Thoroughly squashed, he sat in his corner for the rest of the journey taking no part in the lively conversation, now and again looking at Colin with his hurt spaniel's eyes. The latter, however, was much too full of the excitement of the East-West encounter to pay any attention to him.

CHAPTER SEVEN

Next day, however, Hugh was waiting for him on the platform, so pathetically eager to be friendly, that Colin had not the heart to ignore him entirely. In any case, the other boys soon joined them, and when the train came in, they managed to bag the only empty compartment and hold it successfully against Allan and his friends, who made repeated efforts to storm it. This struggle lasted until they reached the junction.

The main-line train, however, was packed on that morning, because it was the sheep sale day in Blairinver, and so the group had to break up and look for seats in different compartments. Colin found a place and was hardly seated before he saw Hugh's fat, little figure approaching down the corridor. He squeezed himself into his corner beside a large farmer, hoping that Hugh would not notice him. The hope was in vain, as he might have known, for presently he heard him sliding the door open and then the farmers were good-naturedly teasing him and making room for him, and there was Hugh taking the seat opposite him with a smile of satisfaction on his face.

He stared out of the window, pointedly disregarding Hugh's obvious desire to talk to him, but the fat boy was as usual determined to claim his attention. He had one unfailing method of disarming Colin — at least, so far it had never failed to work — to offer him the loan of a book or to press him to accept sweets. Colin had a healthy desire both for literature and for sweets, and little pocket-money to satisfy his appetites. Hugh began to delve into

24

his schoolbag, produced his ammunion, two apples, and handed one to Colin. This time, however, his tactics failed and, surprised and hurt, he said in a loud whisper that infuriated Colin, because he felt it drew everyone's attention to them,

"What's wrang wi' you the day? Are ye no' feeling well, then?"

He pushed the apple into Colin's hand and said very loudly, "Come on, now Col — tak' your usual."

Short of making a scene, and that he knew was just what Hugh wanted, for there was nothing the fat boy enjoyed more than an audience, he could not refuse. Already the conversation had stopped and the farmers were looking curiously at them. In no time at all, Hugh would be playing up to his audience and making a drama out of the thing. To avoid being made conspicuous, he took the apple and laid it on the seat beside him, intending to give it back when they were out of the train, for he was quite determined not to be bribed again. If he was not to be paired off with Hugh for the rest of his school-life, he had to show him once and for all that his friendship could not be bought. The fat boy, however, appeared to read his thoughts and said again, as loudly as he could,

"Fit's a dee wi' ye then, that ye're no' hungry the day? Eat up, Col, and be yersel'."

Raging inwardly, he bit into the apple. Satisfied that he had won, Hugh did not press his advantage. Once more he had succeeded in putting his friend under an obligation. That gave him the right to his company for the rest of the day. For the remainder of the journey he was fairly quiet and that, at least, thought Colin, as he slowly ate the apple that he could not enjoy, was something gained.

The other boys of his class would have waited for him, or at least he saw them lingering at the barrier as he, with Hugh by his side, came over by the bridge. They glanced up, then one of them said something which he could not hear. He was sure that they were talking about Hugh and himself, for the others laughed and then he saw them running along the platform. Of course, there was no reason why he could not catch up with them, he knew that it was Hugh they did not want, no reason except that he had accepted the present of the apple and with it the unspoken pledge not to desert the donor.

He would have kept to the bargain too, at least for that day, if Hugh had not felt the need to justify himself in Colin's eyes for his conduct of the day before. He could hardly believe his ears when he heard his companion's version of the fight. He it was who had come to Colin's aid when he saw that Uisdean was getting the better of him, and he would most assuredly have finished him off if the other West Coasters hadn't attacked him in a body. Colin stared at him, disgusted and incredulous.

"It wasna' like that at all," he said angrily. "and ye know fine ye're making it all up."

"Ye're surely no' denying that I helped you when yon dirty Coaster had ye at his mercy. I got him down, didn't I?"

"Ah didna' need yer help and, anyway, it was a dirty trick. Ye canna fight fair, ye hit him from behind and ye went for him when he was down. And if ye want to know, it was me that dragged ye off, no' the West Coasters at all."

"You're no' meaning that, are ye, Col? I just canna believe that you would do a thing like that. Ah mean, it's desertion to the enemy."

He was so upset by this revelation that Colin realised

that he really had not known that it was he who had intervened to rescue Uisdean.

"It's the truth ah'm telling you and what's more, ah'd do it again."

Hugh digested this in silence. He did not know how to deal with the situation. He had really convinced himself that he had done Colin a service by his intervention and here was his friend not only rejecting his brave deed, but openly confessing that he had gone to the aid of the enemy. Not only confessing, but showing not the slightest sign of regret, on the contrary, glorying in it. Such treachery could not be passed over. It demanded retribution. But what kind of retribution?

He couldn't fight him, he knew what the outcome of a fight would be. Moreover, he had a vague feeling that Colin would have welcomed the chance of giving him a beating. He was not so thick-skinned that he did not sense how tenuous was the basis of their friendship. However he looked at it, he would be the loser. If he did nothing, Colin would despise him; if he fought him, he would get the worst of it; if he broke with him, he would be alone.

He could not bear the thought of being alone. All last year he had been the outsider, occasionally tolerated when he, as he often did, treated the others to sweets or ice-cream. Then as often as not, they ran away and left him, not really intentionally, it was just that the asthmatic Hugh was a drag on them and they were too impatient to wait for him. At school or in the train he made the mistake of claiming the centre of the stage with his performance and his stories, but very soon they tired of that and shut him up. There was no-one who really wanted him for himself. However he tried to persuade himself of the contrary, in his heart he knew that it was so and in his loneliness he suffered deeply from the ostracism. He would have given anything to be like the others. He knew only too well that he was different, not only because of his handicap, but because he was fat and ugly, and even on his best days poor at games.

In class, too, there was little satisfaction for him. He was by no means stupid, but his frequent absences and changes of school had kept him so far behind that he had given up the struggle. Teachers found him tiresome because of his inattention and clowning, and generally ignored him and he, hating to be ignored, revenged himself by imitating them behind their backs. That brought him a little attention from his schoolfellows at first and to him that outweighed the punishments. Besides, to be punished was a kind of distinction. In the end, however, his tricks lost their power to amuse and soon no-one applauded them. Invariably he was given a desk by himself at the back of the room, where he spent a great deal of his time dreaming of how to impress his school-mates, when he was not engaged in creating diversions.

And now when he had, as he thought, won a real friend at last who would listen to him and who had, at least at first, seemed to be impressed by his talk and his performances, and of whom moreover he was really fond, he was turning against him. He had to act quickly or he would lose him for good.

Suddenly he had an idea. Even to Hugh it did not seem a very good idea, and he hesitated before bringing it out. If only, he thought, he had something really big to offer him, so big that it would blot all this out of Colin's mind. But he had nothing, not even a single sweet, let alone anything that would make a really stunning impression. And so in desperation he tried his idea.

"I wonder," he said, looking slyly at Colin, "what the other boys would say if they knew?"

"Knew what?" said Colin.

"Well, if they knew that it was you that pulled me off Uisdean, if they knew that you went over to the enemy. They wouldn't like it, in fact, they wouldn't have anything to do with you. Of course, I'm not saying that I would tell on you, and if they did find out I'd stick by you. I'm sure you didn't mean to do it, maybe you made a mistake, I mean, we were all milling around so it could easily happen, and —" His voice trailed away uncertainly, for he had seen the look on Colin's face and he realised that his tactics were wrong.

"Tell away," said Colin contemptuously, "you're a nasty, little clype as well as a dirty fighter. And as for deserting to the enemy, ye're talking a lot of rot. It was only in fun until you gave Uisdean that dirty punch. And anyway, if you'd waited to see what happened instead of scuttling away, you'd know that in the end we were all good friends. And if you want to know, I think that it's stupid to have a feud with the boys from the West."

"But, Col, there's always been a feud between East and West. They're different from us, they don't like us and we don't like them."

"Who says so? Only someone as daft as you."

"I suppose you want to be friends with Uisdean."

"It's no' your business who I make friends with."

"Well, don't say that I didn't warn you. I wonder at you wanting to have anything to do with that Uisdean MacDonald. He's a rotten type as you'll soon find out."

"Ah'd punch you in the jaw for that if you werena such a miserable coward. An' ah'll do it, too, mind, if ye say anything more against Uisdean. An' another thing, ah'm no' having you hanging around me any more."

29

"Wait a minute, Col. I didn't mean it, honest, I didn't mean it. Look here, I'll — hi, Col! Wait for me!"

But Colin was too full of righteous anger to listen to him. He was finished with Hugh for good and all, he told himself, as he tore down the street and caught up with the others by the school-gate. Soon he had dismissed the thought of the fat boy from his mind.

CHAPTER EIGHT

He had been hoping for a chance to speak to Uisdean all morning, but it was not until after lunch that his opportunity came. The two groups met in the playground and in no time had established cordial relations. Soon they were debating what to do before afternoon school began. Colin suggested that they should go down to the shore, but was overruled by the others who wanted to play football. While they were discussing sides and positions, Colin heard Uisdean say in his slow, deliberate voice,

"I was just thinking that I would not be minding a little turn on the shore myself."

Their eyes met and a flash of understanding passed between them.

"There's a family of cygnets on the firth near the old boat-house. There's at least four of them, maybe more. Ah saw them this morning from the train."

Uisdean smiled a slow, considering sort of smile and said,

"Come on then, Col. We'll just be having a look at them."

At the gate they saw Hugh emerging from the canteen and, for a moment, Colin was afraid he was going to follow them. But evidently for the present, at least, Hugh was not disposed to thrust his company on them. Probably he was afraid that Uisdean still harboured thoughts of revenge. He contented himself with throwing

31

the latter a spiteful look and trotted off in the direction of the playing-field.

When they were alone together, Colin was overcome by a sudden consciousness of his own inadequacy. He could not think of anything to say that would be equal to the importance of the occasion. The more he thought, the more inferior he felt. He would have given anything he had to impress Uisdean as much as he was impressed by him. He looked at him covertly. Uisdean walked easily with a long, loping, almost cat-like stride with his head and shoulders pressed slightly forward in advance of the rest of his body, which give him a questing air. In spite of this slight stoop he gave the impression of superior height. Colin estimated that he must be a good three inches taller than himself. Much broader in the shoulders too, he thought, ruefully aware of his own slightness. In every way, in fact, he was the more definite of the two. His hair was thick and black, and he wore it rather longer than most of the boys, and his eyes in contrast to his dark hair were deep blue, almost violet.

Colin was in every way his opposite. He was rather small for his age, thin and wiry and never still for a moment, whereas Uisdean was slow and deliberate in everything he did. Colin's hair was of an intermediate brown, his eyes changed from pale blue to grey according to the light, his nose had a pronounced tilt to it and his face was covered with freckles. When Uisdean spoke, every word was clearly and carefully articulated with a softening of the consonants and a lengthening of the vowels. Colin listened to him in fascination and, when he did venture a remark or two, he was conscious that his own speech sounded thin in comparison with that of his new friend.

To his disappointment the tide was out when they

reached the shore and there was no sign of the swans. At once he felt depressed. What must Uisdean be thinking of him? He had dragged him down here and now there was nothing to be seen but miles of dreary mud. He stood there staring out over the mud, with such a look of dejection on his face that Uisdean laughed.

"What is the matter, Col?" he said. "You are looking as if something had put you in very bad tune."

"It looks as if ah had brought you down here for nothing. Ah'm sorry, ah quite forgot that the tide would be out."

"There is no need to be sorry about it. Anyway, I should have thought about it myself."

He spoke in so matter-of-fact a tone that Colin brightened a little. He glanced at Uisdean, who was shading his eyes with his hand and looking over the mudflats. All at once he seized Colin by the arm.

"Look over there by the cairn, Col. I am thinking maybe that there is something moving. If we walk along a bit, maybe we will be seeing what it is."

All at once the shore ceased to be a dreary waste of mud and became a magic place of colour and light and movement. Dark brown mounds of seaweed, stretches of green slime and patches where the mud gleamed dully like pewter, rocks of all shapes and sizes, jet-black and clearly edged in the sunshine, and far out the line of the water, blue and silver, with hundreds of waders crowding its edge.

The air exhilarated him, his spirits began to soar. He felt the wind from the sea in his hair and himself so alive and free that nothing seemed impossible to him. He wanted to share his exultation with Uisdean. He searched for something to say that would express the splendour, but he couldn't find words adequate to his feelings. As usual, when he felt deeply about something, he was impelled to action.

"Ah'll race you to thon rock," he said, and before Uisdean had time to answer him he was off, running and leaping, so surely and fleetly that he felt he could race for ever and never tire. He reached the rock well ahead of Uisdean and threw himself face downward, pressing his cheek into the short, rough grass. Then Uisdean was beside him, carefully selecting a seat, and lowering himself with deliberation. Then sitting with his hands resting on his knees, he gazed out at the sprawl of stones opposite, which lay about mid-way between the water's edge and the shore and were known as the Black Cairn.

Colin rolled over on his back and stared up at the sky. His mood of exultation had given way to one of tranquillity. He had completely forgotten why he had come, his recent dejection and his feeling of inferiority.

Presently he sat up and looked at his friend, who was still gazing intently in the direction of the cairn. Feeling Colin's eyes on him, he turned and said,

"Did you know that there is supposed to be a secret passage leading from the castle to the cairn?"

"Aye, ah have heard about it, but it's hardly likely, is it? Ah mean, how could there be under the mud?"

"Well, you see, it would have been made centuries ago before the water covered it. The cairn would have been still on the land then. I am thinking it would have been some kind of fortress that dominated the shore. The story is that when the Norsemen stormed the castle, the defenders retreated along this secret passage to the fort on the firth, and held out there until that, too, was taken and laid in ruins."

"Ach, it's just a heap of stones. Ah think that's just an old tale about it being a fort."

"There is usually some truth in these old tales, else why are they handed down from generation to generation? Besides, why should there be those stones just at that particular point? There are no other rocks out there at all, so I am thinking that they were put there for some purpose. There must have been some reason behind the construction."

"Ah've heard it said that it used to be used by smugglers in the days when this coast had little fishing villages all along it. You can see where they used to be from the remains of piers all along the shore."

"Aye, well, it could easily have been a hiding-place for the smugglers. There are any amount of stories about it. Montrose is supposed to have hidden there and the Covenanters on the run, and Bonnie Prince Charlie, too, but I do not think that that could be true. It would have been under water long before their time."

Colin was silent. He was considering an idea that was beginning to take shape in his mind. He stared at the cairn and the more he looked at it, the more fascinating it appeared, fascinating and at the same time sinister. The long, black sprawl of stones seemed to him like a huge sea-monster asleep on the mud.

"We could explore it, Uisdean," he said. "Look for the secret passage, ah mean."

"You are not meaning today, surely? We would not be having the time for it."

"The tide won't be turning for ages yet, and it wouldna' take more than ten minutes to get there, and we have half an hour."

"It is further out than you think and the going would not be easy. And we would hardly have any time at all for the exploring, for you would have to reckon at least ten minutes to clean ourselves up and be getting back to school."

When Colin had an idea there was never any time lost with him between the conception and the execution. To plan and calculate were not in his nature, he was much too impulsive and now he was impatient to start at once. Uisdean evidently was more cautious. This was a disappointment to him, for he had looked for equal enthusiasm in his friend. As always his feelings were reflected in his face and Uisdean, noticing his change of mood, said:

"That does not mean that I am not wanting to go, but we will have to give ourselves plenty of time. And then we will have to plan it, too, If we do the thing at all, we might as well be doing it properly. So we will just be giving it some thought first."

Colin had to admit that there was sense in what Uisdean said, but he was still a little piqued that his idea had not been accepted at once.

"Aye, that's all very well," he objected, "but when are we going to have more time? We never do have more than half-an-hour at dinner-time, and after school it's the same."

"I know that," said Uisdean patiently. "We will just have to be making a bittie more time and that is where the planning comes in." He spoke with such quiet confidence that Colin was impressed.

"Ye have a plan, then?"

"It could be —" he broke off and stood up.

"We must be off now or we will be late. Will you be looking at that now, Col? Do you see those things moving over there to the left? I am thinking that that is your swans."

Colin jumped to his feet. Coming towards them

36

awkwardly over the mudflats were the two swans and four cygnets. They looked so clumsy out of their element that Colin burst out laughing.

"Don't they look funny waddling around in the mud? Anyway, ah'm glad we saw them after all. Ah wouldna like to have wasted your time."

"It would not have been a waste of time, even without the swans. I wanted to come, and what is more, I am glad I did."

Colin flushed with pleasure. He, too, would have liked to say something in return for the implied compliment, but expressing his feelings directly did not come easily to him, so he said nothing.

Together they ran back along the shore and down the school road, and this time Colin did not try to outstrip his friend, since he no longer felt it necessary to impress him.

CHAPTER NINE

U isdean unfolded his plan to him a few days later. The two boys detached themselves from the others after lunch, and were sitting on a hill a few hundred feet above sea-level, which overlooked the town. From where they sat they had a view over the firth and over the whole length of the peninsula, which thrust itself between the north shore and the mainland to the south. Immediately below them on the far side of the town a long, straight avenue of poplars led down to the old ferry. Through the trees they could just glimpse the black hump of the cairn, now almost covered by the incoming tide.

"I am thinking," said Uisdean, "that we will have to be forgetting about the school for an afternoon."

"Slip the school, you mean? But we'd be found out."

"Not if we choose the right afternoon."

"When would that be?"

"Friday — when we will be having science, because Pipette never notices whether we're there or not."

"What about marking the register?"

"It is Alistair's turn on the register next week. I will be asking him to say 'All present', when he puts the register on Pipette's desk."

Colin was a little doubtful. He was not altogether happy about the deception, nor was he convinced that the plan was foolproof, but, since he admired Uisdean, he contented himself with saying,

"If you're sure you can rely on Alistair."

"Absolutely sure. He is from the West and he will not be giving us away."

"All right, then. Ah suppose it will work out all right. What about the tide?"

"It should be out at one o'clock next Friday according to my calculations. We will have plenty of time."

They sat discussing the details of their adventure until it was time to return to school. On the way back near the foot of the hill, they saw Hugh emerging from the trees. Colin was immediately suspicious that he had followed them and could have heard their conversation, but Uisdean was sure that he could not have reached the top without their seeing him. Not even when Colin pointed out that there was a way up from the north side of the hill would he admit the possibility. And so, against his judgement, Colin let the matter drop.

★　　★　　★　　★

They lay in the sedge by the shore until very faintly they heard the school-bell.

"We'd best wait for a few minutes longer," said Uisdean in answer to Colin's look of inquiry.

"Ah don't see why. There's no-one around," said Colin, who had been itching to start for the last half-hour.

"It would be better for you to be settling yourself," said Uisdean a little drily, for his friend's fidgeting was beginning to try even his composure. "You will be needing all your energy in a little while. We should wait until at least ten minutes after bell-time to be sure that the coast is clear. Noddy may not be past yet. I have noticed that he is sometimes a bittie late in getting back."

Noddy was Mr Munro, the headmaster, so-called because of his habit of bowing his head slowly in greeting when he passed. Colin, in his eagerness to be off, had forgotten about him. There was nothing, he thought admiringly, that Uisdean did not foresee. He settled down once more in his bed in the rushes and for a minute or two stared at his watch.

Presently he said, "Did you know that there's a kind of tern called Noddy, because it keeps bobbing its head up and down?"

"Is that so now?" said Uisdean absentmindedly, for he was engaged in watching the road.

Colin, seeing that his remark had not registered, relapsed into a sulky silence.

Suddenly Uisdean laid a hand on his arm.

"Look, there he blows — in full sail."

Forgetting that he could be seen from the road, Colin was about to jump up to have a look at the headmaster, but Uisdean caught his arm and pulled him down.

"Stately Spanish galleon coming from the Isthmus, dipping through the tropics by the palm green shores," chanted Colin, peering through the reeds at the headmaster, whom he could just glimpse making his slow progress down the road.

"Whist! man, he will hear you," whispered Uisdean.

"Not a chance," said Colin. "He's miles away, not walking the same earth at all. He wouldna hear you even if ye shouted in his lug."

He rolled over on his back and began to drum his heels on the ground. His mood had suddenly changed again, so that he felt reckless and capable of anything. Uisdean watched until Noddy had disappeared from sight before he decided that it was safe to emerge from their lair. Then he set out with his long, loping stride, with Colin bounding by his side like a terrier bouncing along beside a grey-hound.

CHAPTER TEN

Everything exhilarated him and he was constantly drawing Uisdean's attention to something new. Never had he dreamed that a stretch of mud could be so exciting, the smell of it, the feel of it between his toes, the different colours in it, and, above all, the queer little mounds, thrown up by some sea-creatures, that punctured it, seemed to him full of mystery. He clambered over the rocks, not because it was necessary to climb them but from sheer joie de vivre, and splashed through the runnels that criss-crossed the flats.

He picked up trails of seaweed and swung them at the gulls, which were screaming overhead in impotent anger at the intruders. He mocked them shouting back their alarm call at them, "Kar-kar-kar, kow-kow-kow," until Uisdean begged him to stop.

They watched a flock of lapwings rise and perform their patterns, flashing now white, now black, as they dived and wheeled and turned in perfect unison. They came on the family of swans and Colin teased the cob and had to defend himself with a piece of stick, when it came at him hissing and snaking its neck.

As they advanced they flushed a group of oyster-catchers, who rose with indignant cries at the outrage and settled some distance ahead to continue their raking of the mud, stalking about on their long, yellow legs and foraging with busy orange bills. Silent and motionless, amid the noise and activity, stood a grey heron, isolated

41

and suspended as if for it neither space nor time existed. So apparently indifferent was it to its surroundings, that they had hopes of creeping up on it unnoticed, and were surprised and disappointed when it suddenly arose clumsily and flapped away with huge, slow wing-beats towards the southern shore of the firth.

The cairn was considerably further away than it had looked from the shore, and because they had stopped so often to watch the waders, the outward stage of their expedition had taken longer than Uisdean had calculated. Now he urged Colin, who was responsible for most of the halts, to hurry and he, always inclined to swing from one extreme to the other, went racing on ahead, running and jumping in reckless abandon. Suddenly Uisdean saw him stop and heard him give an exclamation of pain. When he reached him, he was hopping around on one foot, holding the other in his hand. Uisdean helped him to a rock and examined the foot, but there was so much mud on it that it was difficult to determine the extent of the injury. He wiped it as clean as he could with his handkerchief. There was a deep gash in the sole of the foot which was bleeding profusely.

"I am thinking," said Uisdean slowly, "that we will have to be giving up the idea for the day. That is a pretty bad cut you have given yourself and it needs seeing to."

"Ach, it's nothing. Ah stepped on a bit o' broken glass. It's bleeding a little, but it'll soon stop if ye tie ma handkerchief round it."

Uisdean hesitated. He was measuring the distance they still had to cover and was doubtful whether it was wise for his friend to attempt it.

"Let us leave it for another day. We must wash that wound in clean water. You do not want it to be festering. Come you now, Col, and I will give you a hand."

But Colin paid no heed to him. He had succeeded in fastening the handkerchief round his foot and was now attempting to run to prove to Uisdean that he was perfectly well able to continue. He was quite determined that he would not give up when they were so near their goal. Realising that it was useless to argue with him, Uisdean followed, but for him the joy had gone out of the enterprise, for he knew that the cut was deep and ought to be attended to. Colin, too, though he was too stubborn to admit it, soon began to regret that he had not taken Uisdean's advice. The salt water, biting into the wound, increased the pain. Soon he was limping badly, though he steadfastly refused Uisdean's help.

Presently he sat down on a rock ostensibly to adjust the bandage, but in reality because a sudden giddiness had come over him and he was afraid that he was going to fall. He put his head between his knees and in a few moments the faintness passed. He pulled the handkerchief, which was soaked with blood and mud, more tightly round the wound and smiled up at Uisdean, who was watching him anxiously.

"That should do it. Another ten minutes and we'll be there."

But it took a lot longer than ten minutes, because by now every step required a great effort of will. In the end, he was forced to accept Uisdean's help, and when at last they reached the cairn he was exhausted and a little light-headed from the pain and loss of blood. He looked at the vast expanse of mud that lay between them and the shore, and a terrible feeling of helplessness and despair came over him.

Neither boy thought any longer of the reason why they had come. For a few moments, they sat on the cairn, Uisdean anxiously watching his friend's white face and

Colin too exhausted to say a word. At last Uisdean said quietly,

"The tide is creeping in, Col. We must not be staying here any longer. Do you think that you can walk if you hold on to me?"

Colin nodded and got up from the rock. His head was throbbing and the ground kept rising and receding again before his eyes. They had gone about a hundred yards when suddenly everything went black and he pitched forward onto the mud.

As consciousness returned, he became aware of something cold and wet trickling down his face and heard the frenzied screaming of seagulls. He opened his eyes and looked up into the face of Uisdean, who was bending over him bathing his forehead. For a moment he lay still, trying to remember where he was and what had happened. Then realisation returned and he tried to struggle to his feet, and would have fallen again if Uisdean had not caught him. Again the feeling of hopelessness came over him. He looked at the enormous stretch of mud he still had to cover and knew that he had not the strength to do it.

"Ah don't thing ah can manage it," he said at last. "Ye better go on without me."

"It is crazy that you are, Col, even to be thinking such a thing," said Uisdean, and though his face was very pale, his voice was quiet and controlled.

"The tide is catching up with us. We'll never get there. Ah'll only be a drag on you an' we'll both be drowned. You go on and get help. If you run you could make it."

He knew that there was little hope that Uisdean would bring help in time, but it seemed of the utmost importance that he should persuade his friend to go. He was to blame for the desperate situation they were in and all that mattered to him then was that Uisdean should not come to harm through him. It was not a question of being heroic, it merely seemed senseless that Uisdean should be endangered too. Besides, he felt so ill that death seemed preferable to the effort of having to struggle over the interminable mud flats.

"I think I have a better idea," said Uisdean. "If I could be getting you back to the cairn. Do you think you could manage that?"

"The cairn," he said stupidly. "What is the point in that? Please, Uisdean, go now, ah'll be all right here until you come back with help."

"Don't you remember, Col? The cairn is not covered at high tide."

"Isn't it?" he said without interest, for he could not see what his friend was driving at. He felt his senses slipping away again and he was too exhausted to care what happened to him. All he wanted in the world was that Uisdean should go and leave him in peace.

"Come on, Col, you must make the effort," said Uisdean, and this time his voice was sharp with anxiety.

He pulled his friend to his feet and half-dragging him, half-carrying him, he succeeded in getting him to the cairn. The next step was to help him to clamber up to the top, and since Colin was utterly worn out this took some precious minutes. Already the tide was lapping round the lower stones of the cairn.

CHAPTER ELEVEN

As he began his race back to the shore, he was tormented by the fear that Colin might lose consciousness and slide into the water. He glanced back once or twice and waved encouragingly, but there was no answering sign from the motionless figure. All at once, another terrifying thought struck him. He had been quite confident that the cairn was never completely submerged, but now he began to have doubts. Any time he had ever seen it, there was always a little black hump visible above the water, but it might be that it was covered when the tide was very high or when the sea was very stormy. He could only pray that he was correct in his surmise. At least the sea was fairly calm and the tide was coming in slowly, so that he just managed to keep ahead of it.

As he ran he considered what he should do when he reached the shore. A few yards along the beach and diagonally opposite the cairn, there was an old building which, many years ago, had been a ferry house and which, he knew, was now used as a boat-house. The door was locked, that he had discovered on one of his exploring expeditions, but once or twice he had seen a boat drawn up on the shore on the far side, tied to a ring which was fixed in the wall. If he were lucky enough to find it there today, that would be quicker than running to the nearest houses. On the other hand, if there were no boat on the beach, he would have wasted precious time.

In the end, he decided to risk it and raced towards the boat-house.

When he reached it, he realised that he had made the wrong decision. There was not a boat to be seen. He tried the door but it was locked. He looked around desperately. It would take him at least ten minutes to reach the nearest house and he could not be sure that he would find help there. He looked again towards the cairn; the water had now covered all but the highest stones on which Colin lay. His eye fell on a beam which had been washed in by the tide. The door of the house he had discovered, in his brief examination, was old. By using the beam as a battering ram he thought he could break it open.

It took all his strength to drag it up to the door, and he was struggling to lift it when he heard a shout and saw a man hurrying along the beach towards him. He ran to meet him and was stammering out an explanation, when the man cut him short and, seizing him by the arm, began to race with him towards the boat-house. Uisdean, still with thoughts of breaking into the shed, indicated the beam, but the man shook his head and said briefly,

"The key is under the rock by the door. You can help me get out the boat."

Together they dragged the boat down to the water's edge and launched it. When they were pulling steadily towards the cairn, the man said,

"And now, perhaps you will tell me what this is all about?"

When Uisdean had finished his story, he said,

"It was lucky I happened to see you from the window. Is your friend badly hurt?"

"A deep cut on his foot. He's lost quite a lot of blood and what with the shock and the exhaustion, he is in a pretty bad way."

"You're lucky that the sea is not rough."

"The top of the cairn is always above the water — that's why I thought I could risk it."

"Generally, but not always."

In fact, in spite of the calmness of the sea, there was not much of the cairn uncovered when they reached it and lifted Colin into the boat.

"The sooner we get a proper bandage on that foot the better," said the man, looking at the cloth which was sodden with mud and blood. "If you could take the oars I could be having a look at it. You can row, can't you?"

Uisdean nodded and took his place at the oars, while the man felt under the seat and brought out a tin box which contained dressings. He wiped the cut clean, dabbed iodine on it and bound up the foot.

"I'll put a proper dressing on it when we get him ashore," he said. "In fact, it might be a good thing to have a doctor look at it."

At this Colin sat up and protested.

"There isna any need. It's as good as new now, thank you, Mr —"

"Ross — Frank Ross. It would be better, you know."

Then looking at the boys sharply, he went on,

"You needn't be afraid. No-one is going to give you away. You were taking a bit of a holiday from the school, weren't you? Perhaps you would tell me what you were doing out there."

"We were intending to explore the cairn."

"And what would there be to explore in a heap of stones?" said Ross drily.

"There is supposed to be a secret passage from the cairn to the castle."

Ross laughed. "That old legend, is it? It certainly dies hard."

"But it could be true, couldn't it? I mean, why would there be a story if there is no foundation at all for it?"

"Because boys will always be imagining things like secret passages and treasure and the like! I know — you see, I lived here when I was a boy myself. I, too, used to go exploring for secret passages."

He looked at Uisdean and there was something in his eyes and in the tone of the remark that followed the scrutiny, that puzzled the boy.

"You didn't find anything of interest, did you?"

"Hardly. We did not have any time to look."

"No, I suppose not."

He said no more on the subject and Uisdean forgot his momentary impression that there was something behind Ross's question. When they reached the shore, he helped him to pull up the boat and fasten it. By this time, Colin had recovered considerably and insisted that he was now able to walk without help. This, however, Uisdean refused to allow. As usual, he had been thinking ahead and now came out with a suggestion.

"Do you think, Mr Ross," he said, "that we could come up to your house? I mean, you said yourself that Colin's foot needs seeing to. And maybe you would be kind enough to let us have a bit of a wash up?"

Ross hesitated for a fraction of a second, and once more Uisdean saw the strange look in his eyes. It was only momentary; next instant he smiled and said smoothly,

"Of course. I was just going to suggest it myself. You could certainly do with a clean up and some dry clothes. Pretty sights you'd look going home like that — apart from the fact that Colin here might catch a chill."

In spite of Colin's protests, between them they carried him to the house, which was only five minutes' walk from the boat-house and situated on a slope beyond the main road.

49

CHAPTER TWELVE

Later, washed and in dry clothes belonging to Ross, they sat by the wood fire, while their host went to the kitchen to make some hot cocoa and sandwiches. Colin was now in high spirits again and, with his foot bathed and bandaged, pronounced himself fully recovered. The only thing that troubled him was how he was to get home in Ross's clothes which were far too big for him, and how he was to explain to his mother what had become of his own. Uisdean decided that he should have his, which after some brushing would be quite presentable, while he, since he was almost as tall as Ross, would ask permission to borrow the trousers and pullover which their host had lent him. Colin, he advised, should tell his mother that he had fallen into the sea which, he said, was almost the truth. This problem disposed of, they began to study their surroundings.

The room in which they were sitting had a long window, extending almost the length of the wall and commanding a view over the whole firth. The furnishings were austere, a plain table, a few chairs, the wooden bench on which they were seated and a sideboard covered with models of sailing ships. In one corner lay a fishing-rod and in the window a large telescope pointing out to sea. Along the wall opposite the window were shelves piled with books which overflowed on to the floor.

Uisdean got up and began to wander about the room, looking at the books, the ships, and finally peering through the telescope.

"I can see the stones you were lying on quite clearly," he said. "There's a black-backed gull sitting on it now. Would you like to be having a little look at him?"

"No, thank you. Ah never want to see a gull again. The brutes were screaming and diving about me all the time. Ah thought they were going to attack me."

"Gulls do not attack people, silly — they are just inquisitive. Maybe they thought you were a curious kind of fish."

"Ah was thinking that they were like vultures waiting for me to die to pick my bones clean. They were swooping down so close that I could see their snaky little heads and their cold little eyes. I hate them, Uisdean — they are evil things."

"What are evil things?" said Ross, coming into the room with a tray of sandwiches and cups of cocoa. He swept some books and papers that lay on the table on to the floor to make room for the tray.

"Col was afraid that the seagulls were going to pick out his eyes."

"That was the craws, wasn't it?"

"The craws?" said Uisdean puzzled.

"The Twa Corbies," said Colin, proud to show off his knowledge. "It's a poem. Ah can say it, if you like."

"Don't let him, Mr Ross," said Uisdean. "He'll never stop if once we let him get started. He is the great one for poems, always spouting them at me."

"Maybe some other time, Colin. Drink up your cocoa now. If you want to get that train you will have to be hurrying. Are you sure you are fit to walk? You certainly look a lot better."

"Ah'm quite sure."

"There is just one other thing that we would venture to be asking you. If you would let me keep your clothes, then I could be lending Colin mine, since they are dry and his are not. We will bring them back tomorrow."

Once more there was an expression in Ross's eyes that Uisdean could not interpret, but again it was gone in a flash and he said with exaggerated heartiness,

"Certainly, you may. You can leave them in the boat-house. You know where to find the key."

"Oh, but we could bring them back to the house. It would be no trouble at all," said Colin eagerly.

Ross hesitated for a moment, then said quickly,

"Well, it's like this, you see. I mightn't be in — I'm out quite a lot you see — bird-watching and fishing."

"Bird-watching? But that is grand! Oh, Mr Ross, would you take us with you sometime?"

"Well, I don't know about that. You have to be pretty quiet."

"I'll undertake to keep him quiet," put in Uisdean and Colin shook his fist at him in mock anger.

"Or fishing then," said Colin eagerly, "that would be just as good. And maybe you'd take us out to the Black Cairn, since we didn't have a chance to explore it today."

"I should have thought you'd had enough of that," said Ross sharply. "Anyway, I told you already there simply isn't anything to explore. It's just a heap of old stones. Besides, it's dangerous — there are holes in the mud you could fall into and disappear for good, so you take my advice and give it a wide berth. You were lucky this time — you may not be so lucky next time."

"All right then, if you say so," said Colin reluctantly, and Uisdean, who was studying Ross's face closely, saw a look of relief come over it.

Was he pleased because Colin and he would not come to harm if they kept to their promise or was there something else behind it? He could not decide and he was still wondering about it when they took leave of Ross, and made their way down the little drive that led to the seashore.

Colin, who was full of the adventure and the visit, was eager to discuss it and did not at first notice that Uisdean's reaction to his enthusiasm was somewhat absentminded.

"He didn't exactly say that he wouldn't take us, so maybe if we went along one afternoon and he happened to be going out, then he might take us with him," said Colin, pursuing the thought that had been exercising him ever since Ross had told them about his pursuits. "Ah mean, he couldn't take offence if we were just there by accident, could he?"

"Could he what?" said Uisdean, who had only heard the last few words of his friend's surmising.

"You havena been listening to me," said Colin reproachfully. "Ah was just wondering whether we couldna just meet him by accident like and then, well, since we were on the spot, it would be hard for him to refuse to take us along with him."

"I was thinking he would not be very pleased to see us."

"Oh, but why not? He was very friendly."

"On the surface, he was. But all the same, I have the feeling that he does not want us around."

"But why? We wouldn't be in the way — we could help him, oh, in lots of ways."

"He will not be welcoming our help I am thinking in whatever it is he is doing."

Colin looked at his friend in amazement.

"You talk as if — as if — well, as if he were doing something that is not right."

"He might be at that, Col."

"Well, ah think you are wrong. He saved my life, didn't he? Ah like him. Ah think he is a decent sort. He didna have to get me off that rock; the fact that he did proves that he is all right."

"It does not prove anything, Col. Oh, I am not saying that there is not good in the man. All that I am trying to tell you is that he does not want us around."

Patiently he explained about the look in Ross's eyes when he had enquired whether they had found anything on the cairn, and about the hesitation when he, Uisdean, had asked whether they might come to his house to clean themselves up, about his unwillingness to have them come back with the borrowed clothes and his efforts to impress upon them the risks they would run if they tried another expedition to the cairn.

Finally, Colin was forced to agree that there might be something in what Uisdean said. He made the concession reluctantly, because he did not like to admit that his friend had been more observant than himself, because he liked Ross and because he was unwilling to abandon his schemes for persuading him to take them with him on his expeditions. However, by the time they parted he was full of new plans, which promised to be even more exciting than those he had originally cherished, and the thought of the adventure to come made him bear with equanimity the scolding he received when he reached home.

CHAPTER THIRTEEN

The fact that Hugh looked at him with a knowing smirk next morning ought to have warned Colin that there was trouble ahead, but his mind was too full of fantasies about Ross and the part that he and Uisdean might play in his unmasking to pay any attention to his former friend. He had by now characteristically swung round to an entirely different view of his rescuer. He was sure that he was engaged in some illegal business and he was determined that he and Uisdean would uncover it.

All through morning school he thought about it and could hardly wait until interval time to discuss it with Uisdean. Then, when at last the bell rang, to his chagrin he had no opportunity of talking alone with his friend, for the other boys came crowding round wanting to know where they had been and what they had been doing the day before. Their absence, they learned, had been discovered and everyone was speculating about the consequences of their truancy.

They were not left long in doubt. Immediately after interval, the summons came for them to appear before Noddy. Very slowly, they made their way across the playground and climbed the stairs to the headmaster's room. As they went Uisdean had time to tell Colin how their absence had been discovered. Alasdair had been sent home sick the first period in the afternoon, and the register had been passed to the next one on the list.

55

"And the next one on the list," said Uisdean, "was your friend, Hugh."

Then Colin remembered the look of gloating on Hugh's face and realised the reason for it.

"Ah might have known it was him," he burst out angrily. "No-one else would have been so mean as to clype on us."

"You cannot be sure that it was deliberate," said Uisdean reasonably. "Alisdair would maybe not have had time to put him in the picture, so we will have to be giving him the benefit of the doubt."

"There is no doubt in my mind, and there wouldn't be in yours if you had seen the look on his face this morning!"

"A look is not evidence," said Uisdean judiciously and Colin, though he was seething with fury, had to leave the matter there, because they had now arrived at Noddy's door.

In any other circumstances, their punishment would not have struck them as unduly severe. They were to be kept in for half-an-hour every night after school for a week, and they were forbidden to go down to the beach for the rest of the term.

After dinner they slipped away from the others and climbed to the top of the hill, where they would at least be able to look at the shore, and perhaps, if they were lucky, catch a glimpse of Ross.

They had plenty to talk about and, as usual, it was

Colin who had most to say. He was still furious about Hugh's treachery and reminded Uisdean of his suspicion that he had been eavesdropping the last time they had been on the hill discussing their plans. His sense of justice demanded that Hugh should be punished and he was angry when Uisdean quietly explained that it would not be justice to punish him, when they had no proof that he had actually spied on them and then given them away.

"In my opinion," Colin insisted stubbornly, "he ought to be taught a lesson. Otherwise he may interfere again in our plans."

But Uisdean was just as convinced that it would be bad policy to make an enemy of Hugh and that would certainly be the effect that a beating would have on him. His advice was that they should simply forget about it, but at the same time be extra careful that they gave him no opportunity to spy on them again. And with that judicious pronouncement, Colin had to be content. Already in their short acquaintance he had learnt that, for all his quiet easy-going nature, his friend could never be pressed into a course of action against his will. And that, in fact, was just as well. The two friends complemented each other — Colin providing the ideas and the enthusiasm and Uisdean testing them, weighing them up and making the decisions.

The matter of Hugh having been settled, they passed to the more congenial subject of the mystery of Ross and how they were to solve it. From where they were sitting they could see the long sprawl of the Black Cairn, and the more they looked at it, the more convinced they were that in it lay the key to the mystery. Colin, mindful of the old stories that it had been used by smugglers in the past, was convinced that Ross was engaged in that traffic, but Uisdean, while admitting the possibility, was not disposed to exclude other explanations for Ross's strange conduct. He could for instance be planning a robbery or, on the other hand, he might be a secret agent on the track of a spy-ring, or again he might himself be spying for a foreign power. He did not think that Ross was merely a common thief; there was something about him that suggested he was superior to that kind of thing. A smuggler he might well be, in it for the thrills more than for the gain, or some kind of an agent, though he could not see what an agent would be doing in so remote an area. As for spying, the same objection held good. What could there possibly be to interest him in this quiet country area? Nothing whatsoever that they could think of. They let the matter drop and turned to the immediate problem of how they were going to keep in touch with Ross and his doings, now that they had been forbidden to go on the beach.

Colin, with his usual recklessness, was in favour of ignoring the prohibition, but Uisdean would not hear of that. Not that he was any more law-abiding than Colin, but he pointed out that it was far too risky. If they were caught or if someone informed on them — and they could not be sure that Hugh might not be watching them — then in all probability they would be confined to the school at dinner-time as well as at four o'clock. Therefore, he concluded, they must observe the ban on the beach, at least for the time being. Later, when Noddy relaxed his vigilance, it might be possible to take an occasional risk.

After he had made this pronouncement he fell silent and Colin, too, after some vain attempts to draw him into conversation gave up, and stared out at the Black Cairn in the hope that he might sight Ross, but there was not a single boat on the whole stretch of the firth and no sign of life on the shore. Then suddenly, he had another idea and urgently he tugged at Uisdean's arm.

"Noddy did say the beach, didn't he? I mean, just the beach, not the shore road or anything else, but just the beach?"

"Of course," said Uisdean patiently.

"So it is only the beach that is out of bounds. There would be nothing against us going up to his house."

"Ross was pretty explicit about not wanting us to go there. Don't you remember? He said that we should put the clothes he lent me back in the boat-house. He'd be pretty angry if we showed up at the house and suspicious, too."

"Yes, but don't you see, we have a perfect excuse for going to the house now? We can't go to the boat-house, because it is on the beach, but we must return the clothes and the only way we can do that is go to his house."

"Well," said Uisdean slowly, "I suppose we could. It's reasonable enough — he could hardly blame us for coming to the house in the circumstances. And quite definitely the house stands well back from the beach, so we would be in the clear there, and we can assume that the shore road is not included in the term 'beach'."

Having thus decided that they were within the letter if not the spirit of the law, they resolved to call on Ross the following day. Then, since they had left themselves only five minutes to get back to school they scrambled down the hill, Colin leading the way with Uisdean following more cautiously, and tore down the road and through the gate on the last stroke of the bell.

CHAPTER FOURTEEN

Next day it was raining heavily and Uisdean advised postponing the expedition. Colin, however, insisted the rain was an advantage since there would be few people about, and especially since there would be little likelihood of Hugh following them on such a day. Uisdean finally yielded to his friend's argument and the two boys slipped away as soon as dinner was over, and were soon splashing through the puddles in a helter-skelter race towards the shore road.

As Colin had surmised there was no-one about and they reached the drive leading up to Ross's house confident that they had not been observed. There they slowed down to a walk, for Uisdean, impeded by the brown paper parcel, was out of breath and needed time to collect himself. Thus at a more sedate pace they approached the house and climbed the steps to the front door.

Colin pulled the bell so vigorously that Uisdean sharply advised a little more restraint. They waited for a few moments listening for the sound of Ross's steps, then when the echoes had died away Uisdean tried again more decorously, but the house still remained silent.

"Let's try the back," said Colin impatiently, and darted off round the house with Uisdean following him. There, too, they had no success and stood about for a few moments disconsolately in the rain, wondering whether to wait in the hope that Ross might return or to give up the attempt for that day. Meanwhile, they huddled in the shelter of the doorway, thoroughly wet and disgruntled.

Suddenly Colin, who had begun to jump up and down to keep himself warm, noticed a key lodged in a crevice between the stones of the lintel. It was a foot or so out of his reach, but with Uisdean's help he clambered up, grasped it, and next second was fitting it in the keyhole. Then triumphantly, he threw the door open and stood in the passage.

The two boys made their way down the long corridor and finally emerged into the front hall. For a moment they stood listening, still not quite sure that the house was really deserted as it appeared to be. Uisdean, in particular, had an uncomfortable feeling that they had walked into a trap and tried to persuade his friend that they should retreat while the way was still open to them. But Colin, who did not share Uisdean's intuition of danger, would not hear of going back now. He announced that he intended to search the house and that if Uisdean was afraid, he would do it himself. Seeing him so determined and reckless, Uisdean reluctantly followed him into the front room.

While Colin searched through the desk, Uisdean watched by the window from where he had a view of the shore road, the beach and the drive. To make quite sure that he would spot Ross he began to rake the shore with the telescope, and when his scrutiny of the beach yielded nothing he turned it on to the firth.

"What do you suppose he needs such a powerful telescope for?" said Uisdean presently.

"Ah don't know. It could be for his bird-watching, ah suppose, if it's true that he is an ornithologist. He certainly has a lot of books on birds and there's some sketches of them among these papers, but that could be a blind. Have you got your knife on you? There's a little drawer here that's locked."

"I really don't think we ought to, Col," said Uisdean, who was extremely uneasy about the consequences of their activities. "It's bad enough to have broken into the house without forcing a drawer. Do leave it be and let us be going, while the coast is still clear."

But Colin had found a key to fit the lock in one of the large drawers and was going through some papers that he had found there. Presently he came to the window with a sheet of paper in his hand.

"Have a look at this, Uisdean," he said. "It's in a foreign language — do you think that it could be a clue?"

"It could be," said Uisdean, giving it a casual glance. "But what use is that if we can't read it? Do put it back where you got it and make sure everything is just as you found it. If we don't go at once, we are going to be late for school."

When Colin had replaced everything as he had found it, and as an extra precaution had wiped the surface of the desk to remove any finger-prints, he announced that he would just have a quick look upstairs, since it would be useful to know the lay-out of the house. To Uisdean's relief he was back in a couple of minutes and, after a last glance round to satisfy themselves that they had left nothing out of place, they let themselves out, replaced the key in its hiding-place and raced down the drive.

They had gone only a few paces along the shore when they saw Ross coming towards them. Uisdean had just time to whisper to Colin that he should leave the talking to him and keep a dead-pan face. Ross greeted them quite cordially and inquired after Colin's foot. Uisdean, in his cool, slow manner, explained that they had been up at the house to return the clothes, since they had been forbidden to go on the shore. He was watching Ross's face closely while he delivered the latter information, and thought that he detected a change of expression, but again it was only fleeting and the next moment Ross said, with an appearance of regret,

"So I shan't be able to take you out bird-watching with me."

"Oh, but you could," put in Colin eagerly, "we needn't go on the shore. We could go up in the woods or on the moor."

"Some time perhaps," said Ross. "Actually, it's the waders and divers I'm interested in."

"You're writing a book on them, aren't you?" said Colin.

"What makes you think so?" said Ross, looking at him sharply.

Before Colin could answer Uisdean intervened quickly.

"Colin is always jumping to conclusions."

"Oh, I see. Well, in this case, he happens to be right."

"For once," said Uisdean. Then, with a little speech of thanks, he handed over the parcel and Ross, saying that he hoped they would meet again when the freedom of the shore had been restored to them, went on his way.

When they were out of earshot, Uisdean said,

"You very nearly let the cat out of the bag, Col. You will have to be keeping a guard on your tongue. I could see that Ross was on to it like a shot."

"About the book? Aye, ah know. Ah nearly let out about the sketches, too. Ah'm sorry, Uisdean, it just slipped out before ah could stop it. Ah really will try to be more careful."

Near the school-gate they came upon Hugh, who looked at them as they went by as if he wanted to say something to them, only they did not give him the opportunity.

63

"Do you think he followed us?" said Col as they crossed the playground. "He looked as if there was something on his mind."

"Maybe he has a guilty conscience, if he did clype on us the other day, and was wanting to excuse himself or something. Anyway, I am pretty sure that he did not follow us. It is more likely he was up the town — there was a bag of sweeties sticking out of his pocket."

CHAPTER FIFTEEN

Next morning when Colin was collecting his things for school, he could not find his scarf. At first he was not greatly troubled about the loss, for he frequently mislaid his belongings, but when he had searched for it at school without result, he began to be worried. He knew that he had been wearing it when they had set out for Ross's house the day before, because Uisdean had snatched it from the peg and tossed it over to him as he was making for the door. What he could not remember was whether he had had it on when they left the house. All through morning school he thought about it, and after dinner was over he communicated his fears to Uisdean. Uisdean thought hard for a moment and then said slowly,

"I don't think you had it on when we reached the school. I remember you hanging up your coat in the cloakroom, but I'm pretty sure your scarf was not with it."

"Ah suppose ah could have dropped it on the way back."

Uisdean considered that possibility, then shook his head.

"It is not very likely. You were running ahead of me and I would have seen it drop. Think hard, Col! When do you last remember having it?"

"I remember stuffing it into my pocket before I started looking through the drawers."

"You did not leave it in the sittingroom; we looked

65

round very carefully before we left. Wait a minute, though — you went upstairs, remember? Could you have dropped it up there?"

"Ah suppose ah could have. If so, we're properly in the soup. Ah might just as well have left ma visiting card for my name is on it."

"Yes, if he has found it. There's just a chance that he has not — yet."

"A pretty thin one."

"Well, it all depends on where you dropped it. Which rooms did you go into?"

"Ah did not actually go into any of them. Ah just had a peep in."

"Hmmm. That is bad. It is very likely that you lost it on the stairs or the landing."

"Ah suppose so. It's just possible — listen, Uisdean, there's one thing ah forgot. Ah did go into a kind of lumber-room. Aye, that's right — ah remember now and, what's more, ah remember taking my torch out of my pocket, because it was sort of dark — there wasna a window in it. It could have fallen out then. Yes, ah'm sure that's where it is!"

"In that case, there is a good chance that he has not come on it. Right then, there is only one thing for it. We will have to go back and get it. There is no other way of it. If he finds it and tells Noddy, there will be an almighty row — he might even call the police in. After all, it is a criminal offence to break into a house."

"Suppose he is in — what do we do then?"

"We have not the time to discuss that now. Just let me think as we go and maybe I will have an idea."

They tore across the playground past the other boys, who were playing football, and past Hugh, who was lingering by the gate and who shouted something after them which they did not catch. When they reached the drive leading up to Ross's house, they slowed down to a walk in order to have time to work out some plan of campaign. Uisdean's suggestion was that they should walk boldly up to the front door and ring the bell. Colin was to ask whether Ross would lend him a book on birds, or at least let him consult it to identify a bird he had seen on the moors. Once inside the house he was to engage him in conversation about this particular bird or ornithology in general. Meanwhile, Uisdean was to ask whether he might use the lavatory, and while he was upstairs he was to slip into the attic and look for the scarf. It was not a very good plan, as Uisdean himself admitted, and it was quite possible that Ross would not admit them. But it was the best he could think of and, since Colin could not produce anything better, they decided to adopt it.

They rang the bell and waited for a few moments, then rang it again and, as this brought no answer, they tried the door. It was locked. Hopeful now that Ross was not at home and that they would gain entry through the back door, as they had done the day before, they went round the house and reached up for the key. It was not in its hiding-place and yet the door was locked.

"He would have been suspicious yesterday and so he will have taken the key with him," said Uisdean.

Colin began to study the house for an alternative entrance. All the windows on the ground floor were fastened, but he noticed a small one higher up which was open. This he concluded from the picture of the lay-out of the house which he had in his mind from yesterday was the bathroom.

"Ah believe ah could shin up that drainpipe, Uisdean, if you would give me a leg-up," he said.

67

But Uisdean had another idea. While they had been standing in the rain the day before, he had noticed a ladder through the open door of one of the sheds.

Within seconds, they had fetched the ladder and laid it against the window-sill. Uisdean held it steady while Colin climbed safely up and through the window, and then scaled it himself. Colin waited only to see him reach the top, then in a flash he was running along the corridor and up the short stair that led to the attic. He shone his torch into the room and saw the scarf at once; it was lying on the floor beside a pile of books. He stuffed it into his pocket and shouted the news of the discovery to Uisdean, who was waiting for him in the corridor. He lingered for a moment or two looking around the attic, but it appeared to contain nothing but some old furniture and empty boxes. He was shining his torch over the titles of the books, when he heard Uisdean calling him to hurry up. At once he abandoned his investigation and, replacing the books exactly as he had found them, he shut the door and bounded down the stairs to join Uisdean, who was pacing up and down impatiently.

"I thought you had fallen asleep up there," he remarked. "What was keeping you then?"

"Ah was just having a look round. Ah found some old books."

"It is hardly the time to be browsing in books. But that is just like you, Col. You cannot resist getting your nose into anything that is printed on paper."

A little hurt at the reproof, Colin did not answer and the two boys, making sure that they left no trace of their entry in the bathroom, climbed down the ladder and replaced it in the shed in the same position as they had found it. They were turning to go down the path when a slight scuffling in the shed arrested their attention.

"There is someone in there," said Uisdean, clutching Colin's arm.

"Ach, it is likely just a rat," said Col and he picked up a stone and threw it into the shed in the direction he judged the sound to have come from. This time the boys heard a stifled gasp.

"That was no rat," said Uisdean.

"Ah'm going to have a look," said Col impulsively, and was about to dart away when Uisdean took him firmly by the arm and led him towards the rhododendron bushes which fringed the drive, and from where they could survey the outhouses.

"Whoever is in there will come out when he thinks that the coast is clear," he whispered.

They crouched down behind the bushes and watched. For some moments nothing happened, and Colin began to fidget and grumble that it would have been better to go in at once and surprise the occupant, until Uisdean put a hand over his mouth and forced him to keep still. Another few minutes went by and then they saw a head peeping cautiously round the door, a large head with black hair, a pale face and thick glasses.

"Would you be looking at that now!" said Uisdean softly. "It is your old friend, Hugh."

"What rotten luck," said Colin. "Ah should have known when ah saw him at the gate that he would follow us."

"We will have to be taking some action or he will be opening his big mouth and telling everyone that he saw us."

"Ah wouldna put it past him to go straight to Noddy. Ah think we should give him a hammering, or at least threaten him with one if he breathes a word about this."

"Hmmm. I do not think that that would make him keep his mouth shut."

"Well, we'll have to think of something pretty quick. He's coming now. Let's jump on him — ah'd love to see his face when we pounce on him!"

"No, we will just be letting him go on ahead, and then we will be catching him up. Now, be sure to behave quite naturally."

CHAPTER SIXTEEN

They waited until Hugh had reached the gate, then still keeping in the shelter of the bushes, in case Ross should appear, they began to stalk him.

When they gained the road, Hugh was about a hundred yards ahead and they could see from the way he was hurrying along that he thought they were in front of him. Walking quickly they began to come up with him and when they had almost overtaken him, he heard their steps and turned round. His eyes, bulging like a startled hare's, darted from one boy to the other. Obviously he was afraid that they were about to attack him.

But Colin and Uisdean merely nodded to him in passing and walked on. Hugh, concluding that no danger threatened him, quickened his step to a run and came abreast, breathing hard with the effort to keep up with them and looking at them sideways from time to time, still a little apprehensive that they might suddenly pounce on him. They went a little way in silence, Uisdean and Colin pretending not to notice his presence, until Hugh's curiosity could no longer be contained and he burst out triumphantly,

"I seen you break into yon house!"

Neither of the two friends gave any sign of having heard him, but Hugh was not to be shaken off so easily. He tugged at Uisdean's arm and said,

"It's no use your pretending. I saw you with my own eyes."

"What do you think he can be referring to?" said Uisdean gently, turning to Colin.

"Ach, ah don't know what he's talking about. Don't heed him, Uisdean."

"You are maybe no' feeling very well, Hugh — suffering from hallucinations perhaps. Would you be saying that he looks a little feverish, Col?"

"You can stop the fooling, Uisdean MacDonald. You know fine that you broke into yon house, and you may as well tell me whatever it is you were up to. Ye've been acting very mysteriously and I'm going to find out what it's all about or —"

"Or what?" said Uisdean, in the same level tones.

"Or I might tell Noddy what I saw."

"You would not like everyone to be calling you a clype, would you now, Hugh? There wouldn't be anyone in the class that would be speaking to you if you did such a nasty thing."

"I won't say a word if you let me in on your secret."

"First he is threatening us and then he is blackmailing us. It is not nice at all, at all, Hugh, and I would not have thought it of you."

"What's the good of all this jabbering?" whispered Colin. "Let's give him a hammering and be done with it."

"What are you whispering about?" said Hugh, and his eyes flickered nervously from one boy to the other. "If you lay a finger on me you'll regret it. I'll go straight to Noddy and then you'll be sorry."

Uisdean's voice was as soft as silk. "No-one is going to harm one single hair of your head. Why should we be doing such a thing anyway? We are all friends, aren't we?"

"You're a crafty coaster, Uisdean MacDonald — but you

won't get round me with fine words! All you Coasters are deceitful, everyone knows that!"

"Now, don't be so hasty, Hugh, and don't you be saying anything that you will regret, and me about to tell you what it was that we were doing."

Hugh looked at him suspiciously, but Uisdean's face was so bland and guileless that he was more than half-convinced. For a few moments he trotted beside them in silence, squinting from time to time at Uisdean and turning over what he had said. He wanted so badly to be friendly with them, with anyone come to that, that it did not take him very long to suppress his doubts of the wily Uisdean. Meanwhile, the latter was content to wait, well aware that his fish was nibbling at the bait. Presently Hugh looked earnestly into his face and said,

"You really meant it about being friends?"

"Why would I be saying it otherwise?" said Uisdean gently.

"Then you will tell me what you were doing? You will let me into your secret?"

"If there were any secret, we would certainly be letting you know about it. But there is not, you see."

"What were you doing in the house then, if you weren't up to something?"

"Well, it is like this, you see, Hugh. The owner is a friend of ours. We go to see him from time to time. Now, the last time that we were seeing him, I left my compass, and as I will be needing it this week-end I had to get it back. And since Mr Ross is away, then we had to climb in by the window — that is all there is to it."

"Imphm. Then you will be telling me," said Hugh, imitating Uisdean's accent, "why it was that you were ringing the bell and knocking on the back door, if you knew beforehand that your Mr Ross was away? I was watching you, you know — I trailed you all the way from the school and you had no idea that I was behind you."

"How would we and you so clever at the shadowing?" said Uisdean, just in time to prevent an angry outburst from Colin, who was seething at the insolent tone Hugh had adopted and the meekness with which Uisdean was taking it.

"I could tell you a thing or two about detective work," said Hugh boastfully. "The way the two of you went along that road without ever once looking behind you just shows how green you are."

"But you see, there was no reason at all for anyone to be following us, so why should we be looking behind us?"

"Oh, well," said Hugh uncertainly, "perhaps — but I must say you were acting most suspiciously — dashing out with a guilty look on your faces and not even hearing me when I called to you."

"We were not —" began Colin furiously, but Uisdean gave him a quick nudge and he relapsed into sulky silence.

"Well, of course, it might have seemed that way to you. I mean, with you having such an interest in detective work you could have drawn that conclusion. But if we had been on any secret ploy, then we would have taken good care that no-one was following us. That is an elementary precaution, as you know — but you said yourself that we never once looked behind. Well, there is the proof for you, isn't it? No mystery at all, just a little errand."

Hugh was almost, but not quite, convinced. In spite of Uisdean's plausibility he still could not see why they should ring the door-bell if, as they had said, they already knew that their friend was not at home. This point he brought out again, but Uisdean countered blandly that they had thought it just possible that Ross might have returned, and with that he appeared to be content.

"You must admit, though," he said, "that I stalked you well."

"You did that all right and no mistake! We would never have known at all, if you had not made yon noise in the shed."

"I knocked against a box when I was trying to get a better view of you."

"Yes. Well, we thought it was a rat, until Colin threw the stone and you let out a yelp. I hope that he did not hurt you."

"Ah hope ah did," muttered Colin between his teeth.

"Colin is just saying that he is sorry that he hit you," put in Uisdean hastily.

Hugh looked at him suspiciously, but Uisdean's face was so innocent and gentle that his doubts were dispelled. He wanted so much to be friends with Colin again, and with Uisdean, too. Since he knew quite well that he could not separate them he was prepared to meet them more than half-way. Already he saw himself included, no longer the outcast that everyone laughed at. He would have liked to ask there and then whether they would allow him to go along with them on their expeditions, but he had the sense to know that to put his request into words would be the wrong tactics. For the present, he decided to be content with what he had already accomplished. He would play it cautiously, and await his opportunity to make himself useful to them.

CHAPTER SEVENTEEN

A t half-past four Colin was impatiently waiting at the gate for Uisdean, who had not finished his detention work. He was still rather cross with his friend because he had been, in his view, so unnecessarily friendly to Hugh and the fact that he was now being kept waiting increased his ill-humour. When he saw him coming across the playground as if he had all the time in the world, it was the last straw, and as soon as Uisdean came up to him, he burst out angrily,

"To see you snailing across the playground you would think ah had nothing better to do than kick my heels here waiting for you!"

"I have not been all that long, have I?" said Uisdean mildly. "I just could not get the thing to come out. In any case, I do not see what all the hurry is for. There is plenty of time."

"That's what you always say. The trouble with you is you never notice the time. Ah'm always having to wait for you and ah'm sick of it — that's what ah am."

Uisdean looked at him in surprise. He was used to Colin's changes of mood by now, but never before had he known him so bitterly angry.

"What is that has put you in such bad tune?"

"Haven't ah just told you? Always having to hang around waiting for you! You're so slow — it's — maddening. Besides, if we're not off the mark quick, we'll have Hugh thrusting himself upon us."

Uisdean chuckled, which only infuriated Colin the more.

"Ah suppose that's what you want! Maybe that's why you're so late, waiting for him."

"If that is what is worrying you, you can set your mind at rest. He will not be coming out for quite a long time. He was not nearly finished when I left."

"Ah suppose that is something to be thankful for."

He was still looking morose when they reached their special tree on the banks of the canal and swung themselves up into the branches. Uisdean waited, idly throwing twigs into the water and watching them float away, until they were lost to sight round the bend or got caught in the tree roots at the water's edge. He knew that Colin's moods never lasted for long. And in fact, in a few minutes, he too was throwing sticks into the water and had soon forgotten his ill-humour in the excitement of racing his twigs against Uisdean's. So intense was their concentration on the game, that they did not see Hugh coming along the path until he was only a few yards away from them. He had seen them, however, and did not wait to be asked to join them. He just took it for granted that he was to be allowed to take part in their game and, ignoring Colin's scowls, he succeeded in clambering up to their retreat. To Colin's disgust, Uisdean even helped him. So there he was, perched between them joining in their game and, what was doubly galling to Colin, his sticks usually won, whereas his own seemed fated to drift into the bank.

It was when he offered to show them the knack of throwing the sticks and Uisdean, instead of squashing him, appeared to be encouraging him that Colin could endure it no longer. He climbed down on to the bank and, ignoring their shouts, he ran off without a backward glance along the path, across the railway line, down the avenue and into the station square. By that time he had worked off some of his indignation and considered whether he ought not to go back. Only that would have meant climbing down before Hugh and that was unthinkable. So he hung about, rather miserably watching a goods train shunting until the other boys arrived.

It was a little satisfaction to him that when the train came in, they succeeded in getting an empty compartment, and when Hugh came along and wanted to join them, they combined to keep him out. The feeling did not, however, last long and was, in any case, little compensation for the uncomfortable thought that he had behaved badly and because of his ill-temper and stupidity might have lost his friend.

CHAPTER EIGHTEEN

Next day, however, he found Uisdean waiting for him after morning school as usual. Nor did he betray by word or look that he had been offended by his friend's sudden desertion the previous day. It was Colin himself who brought the matter up. He had thought of nothing else during the whole of the preceding evening and throughout the morning, and he had come to the conclusion that he had shown himself in a very unfavourable light and had to make amends. This he now proceeded to do and in his contrition even declared himself willing to allow Hugh to come along with them, if that was what Uisdean wanted. To his relief Uisdean said solemnly that he did not think such a sacrifice was necessary.

"But," he added, "we will just be humouring him from time to time. It would be a mistake to make an enemy of him."

"Aye, ah see that. But you don't have to butter him up quite so much as you did yesterday. It was that that made me so mad."

"It was only to allay his suspicions. And after all, he is a poor truachan, when all is said and done. It will not cost us much to be a little friendly towards him now and again."

To that Colin agreed. Now that he had put himself right with his friend, there was nothing he would not have been prepared to do, so magnanimous did he feel.

Thus, when Uisdean proposed that they should do a little exploring of the castle ruins, he even suggested waiting for Hugh.

"It is not necessary to exaggerate," said Uisdean, with his slow considering smile, and Colin, immensely relieved, was off at once with Uisdean following a few paces behind at a steady loping pace. He was in high humour when he reached the castle and teased Uisdean for being so slow, when he finally came up with him.

They spent some time examining the fallen masonry and the arch of the doorway without any result. They were about to give up the search when Colin, who had been busy shifting a pile of stones in the far corner, shouted excitedly to Uisdean to come and see what he had uncovered. It was an iron ring attached to a flagstone. Together they tugged at it, but without budging an inch the stone slab to which it was attached. After several fruitless attempts they sat down on the stones to consider the situation.

"We need tools," said Uisdean, "a crowbar or a pick or something. We will just have to be leaving it for the present. I will see what I can find in the shed at the hostel."

"Ah suppose we'll have to. It is nearly train time anyway."

They replaced the stones and set off for the station. A little way down the avenue they heard a shout and turned to see Hugh running after them as fast as his short legs would allow.

Uisdean, again to Colin's annoyance, decided they should wait for him. Hugh was delighted and chattered eagerly all the way to the station. It was all very well for Uisdean to humour him, Colin reflected crossly, he did not have to put up with him on the train. And, as it turned out, the train had arrived and all the other boys were already seated when they reached the station. Being sale-day too, there were no seats left and he had to stand in the corridor with Hugh beside him until they reached the junction. As soon as the train stopped, he leapt out and before Hugh could catch him, he had joined the other boys. Once more Hugh was excluded from the compartment and his repeated efforts to break in were foiled. In the end, he gave up and went forlornly down the train. Seeing the piteous look on his face, Colin felt a little ashamed of himself and uneasy too, for he remembered Uisdean's advice that it would be unwise to make an enemy of Hugh.

CHAPTER NINETEEN

Next day he rememberd Uisdean's warning again, when Noddy sent for them and they were making their way to his room. They speculated uneasily as they went about the reason for the summons. It could only be that their visit to Ross's house had been discovered and Colin, remembering his behaviour to Hugh in the train, was sure that the fat boy had told Noddy out of revenge. Uisdean's attitude was that they should wait and see before coming to conclusions.

The interview was long and decidedly uncomfortable, for Noddy who was generally amiable and reasonable was extremely angry. "It had," he said, "come to his knowledge that they had deliberately disobeyed him and gone down to the beach."

When Uisdean pointed out that they had not set foot on the beach, he dismissed the objection as a quibble. The beach for him obviously included the shore road and nothing that the boys could say had any effect on him. In the end, they gave up all attempts to defend themselves and stood before him with downcast heads, while he lectured them at length and, when he had come to the end of his strictures on their conduct, pronounced judgement. They were not to leave the school premises after school until train time for the rest of the term, nor were they to go anywhere near the shore during that period. In addition they were to hand in to him an essay every Monday for the same period, and he would enter a bad conduct mark on their report cards for the term.

"At least," said Uisdean, when they found themselves outside the door, "he does not know about our breaking and entering. Goodness alone knows what the punishment would have been if he had found out about that!"

"It's bad enough. It's put an end for good to finding out what Ross is up to and to finding out what's under that flagstone. I wish you'd listened to me, Uisdean, and given Hugh a hammering at the start."

"You are jumping to conclusions again, Col."

"It's no' a very long leap! Who else could it have been? Ah know why he did it, too. It was because he was mad with me last night, because we wouldn't let him into our carriage. This is his revenge."

"Hmm. Did I not tell you to be careful not to make an enemy of him?"

"It's all very fine for you to talk — you don't have to put up with him on the way home as well as at school. And it's all your fault too. Ah thought ah'd managed to get rid of him, and then you had to go treating him as if he was your best friend."

"You know very well that that was all a blind. It seemed the best way of throwing him off the scent."

"It hasna' worked, has it? You should have listened to me at the start."

"We have no proof at all that Hugh told on us."

"There you go again standing up for him! You said we had no proof the last time and that he ought to have the benefit of the doubt. And now you're saying the same thing again!"

"Will you be listening to reason, Col —"

"Ach, you and your reason! Where has your reason landed us? Tell me that!"

"If you would be quiet for a moment and hear what I am trying to tell you. I do not think that it was Hugh who told Noddy about us at all. You see, if it had been Hugh he would have told about seeing us climbing into the house. Surely you must see that, Col?"

"Ah don't claim to know what was in his mind. Whatever he said, he's landed us properly in the cart and that's all there is about it."

"No, it is not, and you have not answered my point at all. There are very good grounds for thinking that Hugh had nothing to do with this and if you were not so prejudiced against him you would see it."

"Well, if it wasn't him, who else could it have been? Tell me that, if you are so clever!"

Uisdean was almost at the end of his patience, but he made an effort to control himself and said quietly,

"It could have been anyone. Any of the teachers, for instance."

"Noddy himself is the only one who comes that way. And if he'd seen us himself, he would have said so. He said, 'It has come to my knowledge,' and that means that someone clyped on us."

"It could have been Ross himself, you know."

Colin hesitated before answering. He did not want to abandon his theory that the informer was Hugh, but he was forced reluctantly to admit the force of Uisdean's argument. He thought over it at intervals through morning school, and by the time the two boys met again, Uisdean found he had come round to his point of view and talked no more of punishing Hugh. But the fact that his sense of justice had made him change his mind did not make him any more well-disposed towards the fat boy.

★　　★　　★　　★

The week passed drearily with detention and extra work and the two boys felt very miserable under the restraint and thwarted, because they could see no way of pursuing their detective work until next term. And next term was at least six weeks away, which seemed to them an eternity. As Colin said, again and again, in the short time that they were now able to discuss the matter in privacy, anything might happen in that time; Ross might complete his nefarious business and escape from the district for good. Turn the matter over as they would, there was no way that they could see out of the dilemma. After three weeks of restriction on their liberty, Colin, who suffered more under the constraint than Uisdean, was ready to rebel.

CHAPTER TWENTY

One bright October day when the sun was pouring into their detention-room and the teacher who was supervising them, seeing them apparently engrossed in their work, had left them, Colin suggested to Uisdean that they should make a break for it.

"He never comes back until five anyway, and we could say that it was five by my watch and that I was afraid that I might lose the train. He was late in coming back yesterday anyway, and I did almost miss the train. That's the truth, Uisdean — I just managed to get over the bridge when the guard blew his whistle, and if the engine-driver had not seen me coming, I would have missed it."

Uisdean thought over the suggestion for some minutes. He was very tempted to agree, but he could see objections to Colin's scheme.

"It is just possible that it might work, but it is terribly risky. Firstly, Pipette might suddenly decide to check up on us and, secondly, one of the other teachers might see us slipping out and, thirdly, he would know when he checked our work that we had not done enough for the hour."

"Ah suppose you're right. But it's enough to drive anyone crazy! It would be bad enough at any time to be stuck in this dreary room, working out those beastly problems instead of being outside, but when we know that Ross is getting off with his little game, then it is just more than I can endure. It makes me want to explode! I

86

don't know how you can take it so calmly."

He was prowling restlessly round the room, looking out of the window facing west from where he could see the other boys playing football in the playground, then going to the one facing east from where he could see the train boys running along the canal banks. He opened the window and leaned out, then called excitedly to Uisdean,

"We could easily leave by the window! It's only a few feet drop to the ground. No-one would see us go then."

"No, Col — it's far too risky. Besides, I have another idea."

Colin shut the window and went and sat on the desk beside him.

"I have been thinking about this, Col, and maybe there is a way out of it."

"Go on, then, let's hear it," said Colin, kicking his heels impatiently against the desk.

"We could go on the Saturday afternoon."

"But you always go home at the week-end."

"I could be making an exception now and again."

Colin jumped down from the desk and began to pace up and down. He was a little disappointed at first that Uisdean's plan did not mean immediate action, but then he realised that the idea had advantages.

"We would have the whole day, not just an hour. Yes, that would be marvellous, Uisdean. A whole long day, we really could do something in that time. And Saturday is the day after tomorrow, so we won't have long to wait. And another thing, Hugh won't be around, so we won't have to bother about him tailing us. I'll ask at home tomorrow and I'll get the usual train in the morning and one that will get me home at eight. Hurrah! That's nearly twelve hours! And good for you, Uisdean — I knew you'd think of something."

"Yes, but not so fast. You are racing away ahead. And before we go any further, just come and sit down. If Pipette comes in and finds you prancing around, you will be in trouble, especially as you have not done one single problem, leave alone the six that we are supposed to do. When we have finished them, we will be discussing the day and the time and all the other details."

Obediently Colin went to his place, got out his book and jotter, and soon his pencil was flying over the page. Normally a quick worker, he got through his problems in record time, spurred on by his eagnerness to return to the fascinating business of planning the Saturday afternoon campaign. With a flourish he slammed the book shut and went to see how Uisdean was getting along. He stood behind his friend, looking over his shoulder and advising him about short cuts in working out his problems, until Uisdean got cross and told him curtly to stop showing off and leave him in peace.

"I cannot think with you breathing down my neck and interrupting my train of thought."

"But you're so slow! Look, ah'll do it for you in a couple of minutes, and then we can talk."

"If you would stop talking now, you would be helping me more than hopping about me like a flea."

At that moment, Pipette came in, corrected their work and dismissed them. Uisdean offered to accompany Colin to the train so that they could talk over their plans. It would have to be the Saturday after next, he told Colin, since he had already arranged to go home first Saturday. This was not at all to Colin's taste, but Uisdean was not to be budged, and seeing him so adamant Colin could only acquiesce.

CHAPTER TWENTY-ONE

It seemed to Colin as if the day would never arrive. But at last it was there, a dry, bright morning, ideal, he thought, as he leapt out of bed, for an adventure. Allan, still in bed, asked him sleepily whether he had forgotten that it was Saturday, and when Colin told him that he was going to Blairinver he sat up, wide awake, and began to question him.

"Ah'm just going somewhere with Uisdean," said Colin evasively.

A few months ago, he would have been only too willing to tell his brother all about it and ask him to come along. Even now, he was a little tempted to reveal something about the adventure just to impress his brother. But he decided against it, remembering how Allan had sternly refused to have anything to do with him in his first few days at school, when he would have given anything to be with him. So while his brother continued to question him, wheedling and threatening, he pretended not to hear. The reversal of the roles, however, put him in excellent humour and he whistled happily as he dressed, which infuriated Allan as Colin could see out of the corner of his eye. At the door he looked back and pulled a face at his brother, then with a warm feeling of satisfaction that, for once, he had got the better of him, he clattered down the stair, making as much noise as possible to annoy Allan still further.

He hurried over his breakfast, too excited to bother to

eat, and stuffing the sandwiches his mother had made for him into his raincoat pocket, he ran out of the house into the bright morning and tore down the road, though he knew that he had plenty of time and, in fact, arrived at the station to find it deserted. He had to wait a good half-hour until the train came, but he did not mind. There was plenty to think about, and besides, it was interesting to prowl about the station when there was no-one around. He thoroughly enjoyed it.

About a hundred yards from the station was the signal and to this he was irresistibly drawn. He had always wanted to climb to the top and since there was no-one to stop him, he was soon scaling the rungs, and reaching the highest one he leant his back on the supporting iron ring and surveyed the landscape from his commanding position. He opened the lid of the little box into which he had seen the porter insert the lantern on winter evenings; then having examined it to his satisfaction, he pretended he was on the crow's nest of a whaler scrutinising the sea for the spout of the great sperm-whale. It was while he was engrossed in this pleasant pastime that he heard a shout and turned to see John the porter gesticulating at him from the platform.

Quickly he scrambled down and sauntered along to the office where John was busy hauling out the boxes and parcels from the storeroom, and putting them on the barrow ready to load into the guard's van. He placated him by lending a hand and as a reward was allowed into the booking-office, where he could watch the preparations for the reception of the train.

The station-master showed him the little cupboard which, when opened, displayed the rows of tickets with the station of destination printed beneath them. He taught him how to change the date on the date-stamp machine and, to his delight, when a passenger turned up at the little window, he was allowed to insert the ticket into the slot and press the upper and lower halves of the machine, then take out the ticket and repeat the procedure for the other end. There it was, ready for the customer with the figures clearly printed on it just as well as the station-master, so he was told, could have done it himself. He worked out the change from a ten-shilling note very quickly and pushed it, with the ticket, through the window on to the shiny, brown ledge, and flushed with pleasure when the station-master praised his efficiency and said he would make a first-class railway-man.

Next he turned his attention to the inter-station signalling equipment, and watched the station-master send a message to the junction, simply, as he thought, by shaking the handle of the instrument, until it was explained to him that it was morse code he was using. Then the needle began to flick, so many to this side, so many to the other side, and it seemed to him like magic when the station-master read the message and noted it down. He was quite sorry when the train was signalled leaving the next station. He himself put the pin into the instrument to show that the message had been received. Then he had to rattle the handle of the neighbouring instrument until the next station put the pin in their corresponding instrument so that the needle in his was fast, showing that they were ready to receive the train. Lastly, he was allowed to run to the signal, pull down the lever so that the light showed green, and put the pin in to fix it there. All in all, it was a half-hour packed with interest and he almost wished he could have stayed there longer, for this, too, was adventure of a kind. He would have plenty to tell Uisdean this morning, he thought, with a pleasant feeling of having accomplished something, as he leant out of the window for a last word with his friends, the station-master and the porter.

He could see Uisdean waiting for him on the other side of the barrier, and he had the door open before the train reached the platform and jumped out while it was still in motion. The guard shouted a word of warning at him for his recklessness as he sped past, but he hardly heard. In seconds he was through the barrier and pouring out a voluble account of his morning's work.

Uisdean, when he was at last able to put in a word, told him that he had already been at the castle ruins, where he had deposited an assortment of tools borrowed from the hostel shed before anyone was up. He, too, had his pockets stuffed full of provisions for the expedition, a pocket torch, some matches and a couple of stumps of candle just in case, he explained, the battery should give out.

"You think of everything, Uisdean," said Colin admiringly.

"Someone has to do the planning," said Uisdean, a little drily, "You get so carried away by enthusiasms of the moment that you do not stop to think things out properly. Now, there is one thing I am going to warn you about before we start operations. If we should find the passage to the cairn, you are to go cannily. No dashing on ahead, mind."

"You sound just like Allan with your warnings!" All the same he did promise to heed the warning and agreed to allow his friend to take the lead.

CHAPTER TWENTY-TWO

B oth boys worked with a will and very soon they had removed the stones, and with the aid of the tools they succeeded in prising the flagstone up a few inches and slipping a piece of iron piping underneath to hold it in place. Next they fixed a rope round it and pulled with all their strength. Inch by inch, they hoisted the heavy slab until at last it was perpendicular, then with a final heave they swung it clear, revealing an aperture about four feet square in the ground. Next moment, they were lying on their stomachs peering into the darkness. Uisdean shone the torch into the hole and Colin shouted gleefully,

"The secret passage! It's it all right, it's the secret passage!"

"It will not be secret for long if you shout the news to the whole town."

By the light of the torch they could see a flight of steps leading down into the earth. Uisdean played the torch on them for a few moments, while Colin waited as patiently as he could until he had finished his inspection.

"We'll have to go carefully. Some of the steps are pretty worn and they're certainly very slippery. I'll go first with the torch and test every step before I put my weight on it. Mind that you tread in my footsteps and take your time about it."

"Right then — let's get going."

"All in good time. First, we will have to cover up the

hole in some kind of way, so that if anyone should happen to come along they don't fall in."

That problem took some time to solve. Branches, which was Colin's suggestion, Uisdean vetoed, because they would not be strong enough. Then Colin remembered that they had passed a house under construction, where he had seen some planks lying about. Laid across the hole they would make a perfect covering, and since, being Saturday, there were no workmen about, it would be comparatively easy to borrow them and then return them when they had finished their exploration. This Uisdean pronounced to be a sound scheme and they set off to fetch the planks.

Their luck held. They met no-one on the way and presently they had covered the hole to their satisfaction, leaving only room enough to squeeze through. Then when they were inside, they covered the gap by pushing the two outer planks into position.

With Uisdean leading, they reached the bottom of the steps safely and found themselves in a short passage, which led into a small square room. Uisdean flashed the torch round the stone walls and into the corners. It was completely empty.

"Do you think it would have been a dungeon?" said Colin. "It feels cold and damp and sort of sinister. Do you suppose there are skeletons buried under the floor?"

Uisdean did not answer. He was busy examining the walls.

"Maybe they used it to keep their treasure. It's a pity we didn't bring anything to dig with. Don't you think we should go back for the shovel you brought?"

"Never mind that now — come here and have a look at this."

"What about it? It's just a stone wall, no different from the other walls."

"That's just the point — it is different. The stones are loose here."

"What is so extraordinary about that? As I reckon, it must be over a thousand years old, so it's no wonder that it should be beginning to tumble down."

"There are times, Col, when you are a bit obtuse. Look, do you see what I am meaning now?"

He had succeeded in dislodging one of the stones and was now shining the torch into the hole. Colin, too, stood on tiptoe and peered over his shoulder.

"From what I can see there is a passage on the other side of the wall. Come on, Col, give me a hand with this."

Soon they had removed enough stones to make a hole large enough for them to squeeze through. The light of the torch revealed they were in a passage about four feet high and three feet wide.

"We will just be going a little bit along it today, I am thinking," said Uisdean. "Next time we come we will take some more candles and some spare batteries."

"It should not be all that far to the shore, that is, if it does lead to the shore. Only about a mile, I should say."

"As the crow flies, yes. But it may be very winding."

As Uisdean had surmised, the passage was very winding, but the boys, once they had started, were unwilling to give up. Even Uisdean seemed now to be caught up by the excitement, and when Colin, as he invariably did, kept urging that they should just see what lay round the next bend he concurred. Soon they had gone so far that he felt it would be wiser to go on to the end, since they had certainly covered far more than a mile. They were beginning to be hungry too, but Uisdean, who was anxious about the battery, would not hear of stopping to eat. He paused only long enough to produce some chocolate from his pocket, and with that to allay their hunger they pressed on, always hoping that the exit lay round the next bend.

Suddenly Uisdean uttered an exclamation and stopped. The ground of the passage, which hitherto had been dry and stony, was soft and in the mud he had seen a footprint. He got down on his knees and shone the torch on it. It was a large print, a man's print, and Colin, who had squeezed up beside him to examine it, said excitedly,

"I've seen one like that before, Uisdean! It's Ross's. Look at the bars on the sole and that little star on the heel. Remember the day he rescued me from the cairn? He was wearing gumboots — I noticed the prints at the time, because of the little star on the heel. I've never seen a print like that before."

"You might be right, Col. The size is about right, anyway."

"Might be right? I know I am!"

"As least we know now that there is an exit to the passage."

"Why? Did you think there wasn't?"

"I was beginning to wonder. We won't be able to go back by the tunnel, you know, Col. There just won't be enough light in the torch, in fact, we'll be lucky if we manage to get there before it gives out."

"There's the candles."

"Yes, I know, but they won't take us very far. We just have to come to that exit soon."

"Well, it can't be far now, Uisdean. There is another thing ah've been thinking. Suppose Ross — ah mean, suppose we were to meet him here?"

"The thought had occurred to me."

96

"He might even be armed."

"I should think that is very unlikely. Why should he be? He would not be expecting to be finding anyone here."

"No, ah suppose not. But then, if he's up to something illegal — and ah'm sure that he is, else why is he creeping about in this old passage? — then maybe he always has a gun on him."

"You will be telling me soon that you saw a suspicious bulge in his pocket."

"No, but it's kind of creepy. Ah just can't help wondering what we would do if we came on him round that bend and he did have a gun."

"You're not scared, are you, Col?"

"Well, no — not really, but ah have a nasty feeling that he might be lurking around somewhere."

"I do not mind admitting that the prospect of meeting him here makes my spine tingle. Anyway, there is no turning back now, Col. The torch is getting very dim."

CHAPTER TWENTY-THREE

They went on in silence now for, as Uisdean said, the sound would carry in the tunnel and give warning in advance that they were there. They were very weary now and it was obvious that the battery was almost exhausted. At last it flickered out and they were left in darkness. Uisdean felt in his pocket for the candles and matches and lit one of the stumps. It was very small and soon the hot grease was burning his fingers. He stuck what was left of it on the end of the blade of his knife, and when that had burnt out produced the last piece. Both boys were now thoroughly afraid and despaired of ever getting out.

A dreadful thought now struck Colin. Suppose when they did come to the end there was another trap-door which they could not lift? He began to remember stories he had read of people who had been immured and died a slow death of starvation. How long he wondered would it be before they were missed and a search party went out looking for them? But no-one would ever think of looking for them underground. There was only the slenderest chance that someone would come on the trap-door. If only he had told Allan when he had asked where he was going. It had seemed such a wonderful secret only a few hours ago, and now he wished with all his heart that his desire to impress Allan had not prevented him from letting him into the secret, for it could mean the difference between rescue and a horrible death. He wanted to communicate his fears to Uisdean and especially he wanted to know whether his friend had told anyone where they were going. But he was afraid to ask. It was a tiny spark of hope which he clung to and which he could not bear should be extinguished.

All at once he stopped. His sharp ears had caught a sound. Uisdean, intent on the candle and the way ahead, had heard nothing. Colin's heart began to beat faster, so that he was not sure whether it was that that he had heard or whether it really came from the outside world. He stumbled after Uisdean, caught hold of his jacket and whispered to him to listen, but he, mindful of the precious candle, was at first unwilling to stop. Presently, however, he snuffed out the candle and stood still straining his ears. Colin had no doubts now — he could hear it quite clearly and never in his life had he heard a more welcome sound.

"It's the sea, Uisdean! It's the sea," he said.

"That is what I am thinking myself. We must be very near now."

Encouraged by the thought that they were almost at their goal, they scrambled on as quickly as the narrowness of the passage and the muddy ground would allow. They could now hear quite distinctly the waves breaking on the shore and the screaming of seagulls. In a few moments the tunnel widened out and ended in a small room in which they saw, by the light of the candle, wooden boxes and bags piled up around the walls. To these, however, they paid scant attention, since all their energies were bent on finding their way out of the tunnel.

"Here," said Uisdean, "hold the light a minute. I think I've found it."

Colin took hold of the knife on which the candle was impaled and next moment dropped it with a yell of pain.

"Now, look what you've done! Why did you not catch it by the handle instead of the blade? It is exasperating that you are, Col."

After lighting several matches, he succeeded in retrieving the knife and relighting the tiny piece of candle. Investigation of the door revealed that it was latched on the other side.

"If we had something to slip in between the wall and the door we could unlatch it. You would not have anything in your pockets that would do the trick, Col?"

Colin after some fumbling brought out a small coil of wire, which he straightened and handed to Uisdean, who pushed it into the crack and jerked the latch upward.

"That's done it," he whispered, "we're through."

Colin followed him through the door and gave a gasp of surprise.

"The boat-house!" he said. "Ross's boat-house."

"A very cunning set-up. He brings the stuff in here by boat and stores it in the tunnel room. A perfect hiding-place for it and an alternative exit for him through the passage should an emergency arise."

"We'd better have a look at what he has got stored up in there. Brandy, I should say."

"In a minute. Let me just see first whether the coast is clear."

The boat-house door was unlocked. Uisdean opened it slightly and peered out. Next second he quickly closed the door.

"There's a boat just coming in and I am pretty sure that our friend Ross is in it. Quick, Col, we've got to get under cover."

"Shouldn't we just make a break for it?"

"That would give the whole show away. He's close enough to see us and if we run for it now, he'll know that we are on his track. Then he'll get rid of the evidence pretty quick and that will be the end of the story; without the evidence there'll be no case against him. No, we will just have to hide in the passage until he has gone."

In seconds they were through the door again and, with some difficulty, succeeded in latching it from the inside. They were only just in time; already they could hear Ross dragging the boat up the shingle and then the click of the boat-house door. By the time he had crossed the floor and opened the door leading into the store, they had concealed themselves in the angle made by the passage and the room. Without making a sound they manoeuvred themselves into a position from where they had a view of the room.

As they watched, Ross brought in a lantern which he lit and placed in the centre of the floor. Then he went out and they heard him dragging heavy objects over the floor of the boat-shed. These he proceeded to bring in and stack round the walls of the store. When he had finished he picked up the lantern, retreated through the door and latched it. Then they heard his footsteps in the boat-house and the door being banged shut and locked.

They waited for some minutes in the darkness before venturing to leave their hiding-place. Then they pushed up the latch with the piece of wire and crept into the boat-house. There they waited for half an hour, crouched behind some empty boxes, until they were sure that Ross would not return.

"I am thinking it should be safe enough now," said Uisdean. "Ugh! I am stiff with all that bending and creeping."

"There is some advantage in being small. You don't have to bend so far! Ah'm no' stiff at all."

"That is fine, then. You will be able to climb up there

101

and fetch down that lantern." He pointed to a hook in the wall out of their reach, where Ross had hung the lantern.

"Right," said Col, "Just give me a leg up and I'll have it down in a jiffy."

"Good!" said Uisdean, when he had lit the lamp, "this is certainly an improvement on candles."

"Aye. It was very considerate of Ross to leave it so handy. Ah wonder what he would say if he knew the use we are making of his lantern?"

"Come on, then. We'll just have a look at what our friend keeps in that store room and then we will have to tackle the problem of getting out of here."

They inspected the boxes; they contained, as Colin had guessed, bottles of French brandy and liqueurs. Next they turned their attention to the bags, which were full of cameras and watches. There were also some small boxes which contained what, to them, looked like a white powder. Colin took a pinch between his fingers and held it to his nose. He was about to lick his fingers, when Uisdean pulled his hand sharply away from his mouth.

"It could be poisonous," he said. "You are reckless, Col — I do wish you would think before you act."

Colin looked crestfallen. He knew that Uisdean was right but, at the same time, he felt a little resentful. Why, he thought, did it invariably have to be he who did the wrong thing? He was very fond of his friend, but just for once he wished that he would make a mistake. It was very hard to be continually told that he was rash and thoughtless, especially as he had to admit to himself that it was true. Lately, it had several times occurred to him that Uisdean was becoming as bossy as Allan and as difficult to impress.

Still, he did have his moment when they had finished their inspection and were turning their attention to getting out of the boat-house. It was he who pointed out that the double door could be opened from the inside simply by pulling up the bolt that held one side of the door at the bottom and pulling down the corresponding bolt that held it at the top. Then all they had to do was to lock it with the key, which they found under the stone. In about a quarter of an hour they were back where they had started in the castle ruins and had put the slab in position again. It remained only for them to replace the stones and carry back the slabs of wood which they had borrowed. This, too, they accomplished without mishap.

CHAPTER TWENTY-FOUR

The question which they debated over and over again, during the days which followed, was whether they should inform the police of their discovery or whether they ought to wait until they had found out where Ross got the stuff from, and who else was involved in the smuggling. The latter was by far the most attractive proposition, particularly to Colin who pointed out that, since they had embarked on the adventure, they should see it through to the finish. If they handed it over to the police, then they would have no further part in it. To go it alone, at least until they found out more, was what he urged. In the final stages, of course, they would have to bring in the police, but to do so now would be such a tame ending to their splendid adventure that he could not bear to contemplate it. Besides, the fame, and perhaps the reward, that would be theirs would be far greater if they solved the whole business.

They were sitting on top of the hill, looking at the sea through a pair of old binoculars that Uisdean had brought back with him from home. And while they kept an eye on the water for Ross, they argued as they had been doing all week whether they should report their discovery.

"It's like this," said Uisdean, whose turn it was to keep watch, "unless we do something soon it may be too late. We will not be free to go down to the shore until next term, and by that time Ross may have left the country."

"Maybe we could go next Saturday."

"I thought you said that your mother was so angry last

time, because of the mess you got your clothes in, that she would not allow you to go again?"

"Aye, she was. But she may have simmered down by next week, though ah have my doubts about that."

"If we do not think of something soon, then we will just have to be reporting it."

"Oh, Uisdean, no! Just imagine handing the thing over to Roller. He'd be sure to bungle the whole thing up."

"Yes, that is true. He would be no match for Ross and he'd be sure to want to do the whole business himself in order to get the credit and the promotion."

Roller, so-called because of his peculiar swaying gait, was not a popular figure with the boys. They had come up against him too often in their pursuits and the encounters had not engendered respect on either side.

Uisdean handed the glasses to Colin, who focused them and in his turn began to search the stretch of water. So occupied, he fell silent and Uisdean, too, stared out thoughtfully at the firth until, mesmerised by the rise and fall of the waves, he forgot the present and felt oddly relaxed and at peace. All at once, an exclamation from his companion partially recalled him to reality.

"There's a big ship just coming in to Inverton," Colin said.

"Is there?" said Uisdean. "What nationality?"

"Ah can't tell from here. Ah canna see her flag plainly enough. Ah think she's anchoring. She will likely be waiting for the tide." After a pause, he said excitedly,

"There's a boat being launched! Two boats!"

"Let's have a look."

Colin did not answer. His attention was held by the boats, one of which was obviously making for Inverton, while the other was heading westwards along the firth. At last he handed the binoculars to Uisdean.

"Take a look at that boat," he said. "Ah canna think why it should be coming up the firth instead o' going into port."

Uisdean watched it for some time, then handed the glasses back to Colin.

"It could be making for the Black Cairn, Col."

Colin was so excited that he could hardly focus the binoculars. At last he picked up the boat. There was no doubt about it; it was heading straight for the cairn. As he watched, it disappeared from his view behind the cairn.

"She's gone out of sight," he said. "No — wait a minute, ah can just see the end of the prow. She's stopped there."

For ten minutes they took it in turn to watch the cairn, until they saw the boat move out of the shelter of the stones and head back eastwards towards the ship."

"Ah'm sure she was unloading something," said Colin.

"They might just have been having a look at it. Maybe it caught their attention when they were coming in, and having nothing better to do with their time, they were curious and went to investigate it."

"You are always pouring cold water on my ideas, but ah know that I am right."

"I was only pointing out another possible explanation to you."

"Well, ah think that your possible explanation is an impossible one. It doesna make sense at all. Now, what would make sense is that they were unloading the goods for Ross."

"The same thought had occurred to me."

"Why couldn't you say so then, instead of making out you were so superior?"

"Because it is not right to take the explanation that suits you best. And that is what you are always doing, Col. You have to keep an open mind until you are in possession of all the facts."

"You sound like Pipette. Anyway, ah'll bet you anything you like that ah'm right."

"I would not be putting more than a shilling on it myself."

"Done then! And you can say goodbye to that shilling right now!"

"I would not say but that you are right, Col, but we will just wait and see."

"That's just the point — we canna wait. Oh, blast Noddy! If it werena for him we could go out to the cairn after school and see for ourselves. What do you say, Uisdean, are you game to do it? After all, this is an emergency, in fact, it is our duty to go. That's how ah see it, anyway, and if we do find that that's where he gets the stuff, then they'll be so grateful to us that there'll be no word about disobeying Noddy and all that stuff. Ah'm no' scared anyway — ah vote we go today."

"It is not a question of being scared. You are forgetting (a) that the tide will be full in at four o'clock, and (b) that we could easily be seen from the house and (c) that Ross himself might very well be rowing out to collect his haul."

"All right, then, since you think of everything, what do you suggest we should do?"

"Suppose we were to go at night —"

"At night! But how could ah? It's all very well for you, you're on the spot."

"Well, this is what I was thinking. Next Friday is the school concert. Supposing you were to ask permission to stay the night at the hostel. Noddy is very keen on the concert; I am thinking he would agree."

"Even though we are in disgrace?"

"Noddy is pretty fair. He would not punish you further

by depriving you of the treat. Anyway, it is worth trying. You can say how disappointed you would be to miss it and how there is no train or bus that would get you home. My own opinion is that he will be so impressed by your keen interest in his concert, that he will not make any difficulties. Come on, Col, we had better run for it."

They reached the school gates just as the bell was ringing. As they crossed the playground, they saw Hugh coming towards them and Colin had just time to whisper to Uisdean that he would go to see Noddy at four o'clock, before he came up with them.

CHAPTER TWENTY-FIVE

While Uisdean was waiting at the door for Colin, Hugh came out. His face lit up when he saw Uisdean. Generally he was so late in getting out that all the others had gone, and he could never catch up with them with his short legs and his asthma. But this time he was really in luck. He would have Uisdean's company and that was almost as good as being with Colin.

"You don't mind if I come with you?" he said, beaming all over his heavy face.

"But I am not going anywhere at all. I am just waiting for Colin."

"That's fine. I'll wait with you, then. I'm not in any hurry."

Uisdean, being easy-going and a little sorry for the outcast, would have tolerated him, only he knew that Colin would be anything but pleased when he came out and found that Hugh had imposed himself on them.

"Well, I do not know how long he will be. So maybe you had better be getting along. There is no good in two of us hanging about waiting. Anyway, we have detention after this."

"Oh, but I'd be glad to keep you company until then. It isn't any trouble at all," said Hugh, so eagerly that Uisdean had not the heart to tell him bluntly to take himself off.

"Where is he, then?"

"He is just up seeing Noddy about something," answered Uisdean, and immediately he regretted that he had let the information slip out, for he saw by the way the fat boy's eyes lit up that he had sensed that he was concealing something.

"What's he been up to then?" said Hugh, his nose twitching with curiosity.

"Nothing, so far as I know," answered Uisdean, as casually as he could. But Hugh was not to be thrown off the scent.

"What's he doing seeing Noddy then?"

"It is you that are the inquisitive one."

"It isn't a secret, is it? You needn't be so close about it. You are always acting so mysteriously you two, and, after all, remember you did promise that if you did have a secret, you would let me in on it."

"And so I would, if there were — but there isn't."

"Well, then, why can't you tell me?"

Knowing that he would cling like a burr until he told him, Uisdean yielded in the hope that he would get rid of him.

"He is just asking permission to stay in the hostel on Friday night after the school concert."

"I wish I had thought of that. I'd love to come, too."

"Oh, well," said Uisdean hastily, "it was just an idea he suddenly had. I do not suppose it will come to anything. I was hearing that we are pretty full up, so as likely as not there will not be room."

At this point, Colin came runnng over the playground and Uisdean walked towards him, saying over his shoulder that they had to go now or they would be in trouble for being late for detention. The persistent Hugh was not to be shaken off so easily. He trotted after them and catching them up at the door, peered up inquisitively

110

into Colin's face and said,

"How did you get on with Noddy?"

"All right," said Colin.

"Is he letting you stay?"

Colin threw a look of exasperation at his friend. It was bad enough to come out and find that Uisdean had allowed himself to be taken over by Hugh. To discover that he had also been discussing his business with him was infuriating.

"You might tell us," persisted Hugh.

Colin was about to tell him what he thought of his interference, when he caught a warning look from Uisdean and, with difficulty, controlled himself.

"I wouldn't mind going to Noddy myself and asking if I could stay too."

"There won't be room for you."

"If there is for you, why can't there be for me?"

"Ah never said there was. Noddy just said that he would see. We'd better get a move on, Uisdean, we're late as it is."

Hugh called after them, "Well, you can't stop me asking, anyway."

CHAPTER TWENTY-SIX

In fact, he had asked and been given permission to stay, as they discovered when they found him waiting for them at the door after the concert. He beamed at them triumphantly and, ignoring Colin's scowl, addressed himself to Uisdean.

"I asked if I could be put into your dormitory. I hope you don't mind."

"It is not a question of my minding. It will be a question of whether there will be enough room."

He chattered incessantly all the way to the hostel, too carried away by the sound of his own voice to notice their lack of response.

"Go up to the wash-room as soon as we get there," whispered Uisdean, while Hugh was engaged in demonstrating how much better he could have done an item in the concert programme.

"If he's in with us we may as well call the whole thing off," muttered Colin.

"We will just have to chance it," said Uisdean.

"What are you whispering about?" said Hugh, suddenly becoming aware that his performance had no audience.

"Nothing — nothing at all," said Uisdean hastily. "It is yourself that is the good mimic, Hugh, you should have been on that platform tonight."

When they reached the hostel, Hugh went to find out from the matron which dormitory he had been allotted to.

"It all comes of your being so friendly to him," said Colin angrily, when they were alone. "He actually thinks that we want him around and it is all your fault."

"I have told you," said Uisdean patiently, "that it is better than he should think he is our friend than that he should become our enemy. Anyway, it is no time for us to be arguing about what I should or should not have done. What we have to do is to decide whether we should go ahead with our plan, if by bad luck he should be in the same dormitory."

"He's sure to be. You heard what he said. He asked to be put in with you."

"I think myself," said Uisdean, ignoring his friend's ill-humour, "that whatever happens we must go tonight. We will be hoping that he is a heavy sleeper."

"Ah wish we could put something in his cocoa, some drug to make sure that he doesn't wake up."

"Well, we can be doing no such thing, so what is the use of talking about it? Now listen, Col, while I go over the plan again."

"Ach, you don't need to. Ah know all the details. You get up when you are sure that everyone is asleep, slip out to the wash-room, where you wait for me. In a few minutes, I follow you there. Then we creep downstairs to the cloak-room and make our exit through the window. You are sure that it is big enough, ah suppose?"

"Quite sure — I have tried it. Well, I think that everything is quite clear."

"Ah suppose so."

"Mind that you do not drop off to sleep yourself."

"Ah'm no' likely to."

"Right then — we had better be getting back or there will be no cocoa and buns left for us."

Hugh, who had been watching the dining-room door,

came hurrying over to meet them with a broad smile on his face.

"It's all right. I've fixed it," he said. "I am to be in the same dormitory as you. Isn't that fine? I have some conjuring tricks that I can show you."

"Another time, Hugh," said Uisdean. "Tonight I am so tired that I could be sleeping right here where I am standing."

"Oh, well then —"

"Me, too," said Colin. "Ah'm so exhausted ah think ah'll get into bed right away."

"But I've saved you some cocoa and some rolls."

"Thanks, ah'm no' hungry."

"Oh, well then, I expect that we will manage your share between us, eh, Uisdean?"

"I do not think that I am wanting anything either. Look, you eat it yourself, Hugh. We will be going up and we will see you later."

For a few seconds, Hugh hesitated. His face reflected the conflict between his desire to be with them and his stomach. The latter won and he hurried off to devour the buns and cocoa. Meanwhile, Uisdean and Colin raced upstairs, and by the time Hugh appeared they were in bed with their pyjamas over their clothes, their eyes shut and they were breathing deeply and regularly as if they were asleep. Hugh came over, and after a few vain attempts to waken Uisdean, he retreated to his own bed at the other side of the dormitory. For a while they heard him trying to draw the other boys into conversation, going through the repertoire they knew so well. But since most of the others, too, were acquainted with the fat boy's performances, their interest soon flagged and they drifted away to bed. Deprived of his audience, Hugh soon settled down to sleep, and when the prefect came to put out the lights the room was already very quiet.

Colin lay listening to the sounds from the house, the rattle of crockery from the kitchen, the creak of a stair, distant laughter, the closing of a door. As his eyes became used to the darkness, he was able to pick out the objects in the room. He would be able to make his way to the door without using his torch. He felt under the bed to make sure that he had put his shoes and raincoat there. Reassured on that point, he settled down to wait with his eyes on Uisdean's bed, which was close to the door.

The minutes crawled by and still Uisdean made no move. He switched on his torch under the bedclothes to look at his watch, and was astonished to find that it was only eleven o'clock. A whole hour yet to wait! He sat up in bed and looked around him. A sliver of moonlight fell through a chink in the curtains. He watched it move slowly over the floor for a few moments, then he lay down again and fixed his eyes on Uisdean's bed. Suddenly he started up in alarm. Someone had spoken close beside him. He strained his ears and again he heard the voice, an unintelligible muttering from the next bed. "Someone talking in his sleep," he said to himself, and relaxing again, he snuggled back into the warmth of the blankets.

Presently the sounds inside the house died away. Outside, too, it was very quiet. Occasional footsteps in the street echoed into the room and receded into the night. All at once, there came an unearthly wailing from directly under the window, an eerie screaming and snarling and scuffling that made every nerve in his body tingle. It faded, then came again, this time wilder and more furious, until he was certain that it could not have failed to waken everyone in the room. He looked around, but

115

there was no movement from the beds, and then he smiled at his own fright, realising that the sounds he had heard were nothing more sinister than tomcats brawling in the bushes below. He lay down again listening to the regular breathing, punctuated by an occasional snore, from his companions. The warmth of the bed and the strain of keeping his eyes fixed on Uisdean's bed were making him drowsy.

All at once he started up. He must have drifted off to sleep and someone was shaking him awake. Bewildered and not realising for the moment where he was, he opened his mouth to speak, but a hand was placed over it stifling the sound and a voice, Uisdean's voice, whispered,

"Hurry up, Col! Get your shoes and coat and come on!"

Still half-asleep, he felt under the bed for his bundle, put his pillow under the bedclothes in case anyone should wake up and notice the bed empty, and picked his way cautiously to the door. Uisdean was already half-way down the stairs. Very carefully he tiptoed after him and, in a few moments, had reached the cloakroom, where Uisdean had already opened the window and was climbing on to the sill.

"It is about six feet to the ground," he whispered. "When you get out, pull the window down, but do not shut it completely."

CHAPTER TWENTY-SEVEN

They ran through the silent streets, occasionally dodging into a doorway when they thought they heard footsteps. In fact, they met no-one, the town was deserted and very soon they had left it behind and were on the road that led to the shore. As they came near Ross's house, they stopped for a moment and looked up at it. It was in darkness except for one room, where light was showing through a gap in the curtains.

"That's Ross's bedroom," said Colin. "He must be going to bed."

They took off their shoes and stockings and hid them behind a rock near the boat-house, then they set out over the mud-flats. Everything seemed so strange to them, transformed by the night. Shapes, sizes and colours were all so different from the daytime, and the whole shore and firth were so eerily quiet without the gulls screaming and wheeling over their heads, that they, too, felt subdued and talked little and that only in whispers. There was a wind which blew the clouds over the moon, so that the light was fitful, which made the going difficult. They passed the family of swans, headless and unfamiliar in their sleep, and were startled when some oyster-catchers rose suddenly out of the shadow of a rock and fled with shrill scolding towards the southern shore of the firth.

When they were about half-way there, they stopped for a brief rest. Seated side by side on a rock, they surveyed the distance they had come and the stretch they still had to cover. Suddenly Colin clutched Uisdean's arm.

"Look!" he said, "There's a light in Ross's house and it's the sittingroom this time, so he has not gone to bed."

All at once they felt very small and exposed perched on their rock in the vast expanse of mud-flats and, for the first time, though neither put his thoughts into words, they began to have doubts about the wisdom of tackling the business alone. As they watched, they saw the light go out and the house became a dark, brooding shape overlooking the shore and the flats. The wind was stronger now and the moon gave very infrequent light for there were dark, heavy clouds scudding across the sky. Colin shivered and clambered down on to the mud.

"It's getting cold," he said, "I think we'd better push on."

"Yes," said Uisdean, "it will not be very long before the tide turns."

"No Ross to rescue us this time if we get cut off."

"He would be wishing that he had left you on the cairn, if he knew what we were up to now!"

"Do you know, Uisdean, ah had the queer feeling when ah was sitting on that rock, that he could see us."

"It is you that has the imagination! How could he be seeing us and it so dark?"

"Ah suppose you're right. It's just that when the moon comes out —"

"In the few little blinks of moonlight there have been since we left the shore, I would say that it is highly unlikely."

"How long do you think it will take us now?" asked Colin, after they had trudged on for some time in silence.

"Not more than ten minutes," I should say."

"It does not seem to be getting nearer."

"Distances are difficult to judge in this light."

"It looks like a great black panther sprawling out there in the dark. I have the feeling that it is just waiting to pounce on us."

Uisdean laughed. "It is you that are fanciful, Col, and all about an old heap of stones!"

"Ah know that. All the same, it looks sinister, sort of brooding and watchful."

"First it was Ross and now it is the cairn that is keeping its eye on us."

Colin glanced uneasily in the direction of the house. There was not a glimmer of light to be seen anywhere.

"What are we going to do when we get there?"

All at once the whole enterprise seemed futile to him. The night and the vastness of the firth made him feel very small, and in spite of himself he could not help remembering the dread of his last experience on the flats. Besides, how could they, two schoolboys, with nothing to help them but their hands and a pocket torch, find anything in the great mass of stones at dead of night? But he said nothing of his apprehensions to Uisdean, who was covering the ground now with his long, loping stride at such speed that Colin had to run to keep up with him.

"Do you mind about the holes Ross told us were near the cairn?" he asked presently. "Do you think that there is anything in what he said?"

"No, of course not. You know fine that was only to keep us away."

They started their investigation on the far side of the cairn, because that was where the boat had been on the day they had watched it from the hill. They examined first the base and then the sides, without finding anything of note.

"It is foolish that we are," said Uisdean. "If there is a hiding place, it is far more likely that it is near the top, in

119

the part that is not covered when the tide is in."

"Give me a leg up then," said Colin, "This is my speciality."

With Uisdean's help, Colin scrambled up on to the top of the cairn and began his investigation. In a few moments, he called down urgently,

"Uisdean, come here, quick!"

With some difficulty, because he was less skilled in climbing than Colin, Uisdean succeeded in joining his friend on the summit of the cairn.

"You have found something, then?" he said.

"No, not yet. Look! right opposite — there's a light on the shore."

Uisdean looked in the direction his friend indicated.

"I cannot see any light at all."

"It's gone now."

"Perhaps it was a will o' the wisp, Col."

"I tell you there was a light! Ah have eyes in my head, haven't ah? Ah suppose you think that ah imagined it."

"It might have been the moonlight glinting on a piece of broken bottle or something."

"It was nothing of the sort. It was a moving light like as if someone was walking along the shore with a torch. It was just for a few seconds and then it went out. Ah know ah'm right."

But Uisdean thought he had only imagined it.

"Well, never mind. We had better get busy."

On hands and knees they crawled over the top of the cairn, searching under the stones for the hiding-place, until finally they had to admit defeat. Uisdean was the first to climb down. Colin followed him, but the stone which he had chosen as his first foothold slipped away and he was left clinging with his hands to the top. Uisdean went to his aid and was about to guide his foot to a fresh hold, when Colin said breathlessly,

"Ah'm going up again. Just give me a heave up."

Uisdean did as he asked and waited while Colin felt among the stones at the spot where he had just been clinging to the cairn.

"Could you come up?" he said presently. "Ah canna manage to move this one by myself."

Next moment, Uisdean was kneeling beside him on the top of the cairn.

"Ah think there's something under this stone. It moved when ah was holding on to it — sort of swung up an inch or two, and then back again when ah let go of it. If you would take that side, ah'll take the other, and maybe we can lift it out."

Together they succeeded in raising the stone, and Uisdean shone the torch into the cavity beneath.

"There is something at the bottom," he said. "If you hold the torch for me, I will climb down."

"Best let me go. Ah'm thinner than you and lighter, and less likely to bring the stones tumbling down on top of me."

It was only about six foot to the bottom, an easy climb for the nimble Colin.

"There's a sack and a couple of cases and a small tin box."

"Heave up the tin, so that I can get a grip on it."

"Right — coming up."

"Good! I have got it. And now I will give you a hand."

They sat on the stones for a few moments with their prize beside them, exultant at their success. Colin was anxious to examine the contents on the spot, but the box was securely fastened with metal bands, which they could not remove without pliers.

"We might manage it with your knife, Uisdean," he said.

"We might, but it would take some time and time is what we have not got. You will just have to be patient. Let's get down now. You go first and I will hand the box down to you."

★　　★　　★　　★

They reached the shore without mishap, retrieved their shoes and stockings and put them on. In all, their enterprise had taken them an hour and a half. Now that it was successfully accomplished, they had forgotten their initial apprehensions and caution, and were so absorbed in talking about their find that all thought of danger was far from their minds. Colin, too, no longer remembered the light he had seen on the shore when he was on the top of the cairn, and ran along beside Uisdean, who was striding out at a brisk pace for home.

It was quite dark now, with a heavy, cloudy sky that completely concealed the moon. The wind blew in sudden little gusts that made them shiver and pull their coat collars up round their neck and ears. They took turns in carrying the box, not because it was heavy, but because each wanted to have a hand in bringing home the prize. They had decided that they would hand it over to Noddy in the morning. He would be bound to hear sooner or later about their exploit, so it would be better for them to tell him themselves. He would scold them, of course, for disobeying his instructions, but they were sure he would be pleased with them when he realised they had helped to bring a criminal to justice.

"Won't Hugh stare when he sees us with the box in the morning," said Colin. "Ah bet he's snoring away peacefully and —"

He did not finish his sentence. He had just time to see

the figure of a man rising from a clump of whin-bushes they were just passing, and to shout a warning to Uisdean. Then something heavy hit him on the back of the head, he heard Uisdean cry out and then he felt himself falling down — down — down — into a deep black chasm.

CHAPTER TWENTY-EIGHT

When consciousness began to return, Colin found himself lying on a surface that felt hard and damp to the touch. He tried to lift his head, but such a stab of pain shot through it that he sank back with a groan. He lay for a few moments until the pain receded and then cautiously raised his head again. As his eyes grew accustomed to the darkness, he began to make out the shapes of the objects near to him. All at once, he realised where he was. He was lying on the floor of the boat-shed with his hands and feet tied. At first he thought that he was dreaming, but gradually recollection returned.

He struggled into a sitting position and looked around for Uisdean, but there was no sign of his friend. His first feeling was one of desolation, but then a consoling thought occurred to him. He remembered shouting a warning to Uisdean, so it was possible that he had escaped and gone to bring help.

He lay still for a little considering the situation. The pain in his head was more bearable when he closed his eyes and lay quiet. He must have dozed off, for when he opened his eyes again, it was almost light in the shed. Though his hands and feet were so numb that they did not seem to belong to him, and his head still hurt when he moved it, he tried to roll himself over the floor in the direction of the door. Between him and his goal lay a boat, so that he had to skirt it in order to reach the door. Inch by inch, he edged himself along, resting frequently when the pain and the effort became too much for him.

After what seemed to him hours in his semi-conscious state, he rounded the prow of the boat and sank back exhausted on the floor. He must have drifted off again into unconsciousness, for when he regained his senses, he could see the sun shining in through the cracks in the shed. He set his teeth and forced himself to cover the remaining few yards in a state of near desperation, for he knew now that Uisdean could not have escaped or he would have brought help long since. He must, he calculated, for he had forgotten to bring his watch, been lying for nearly five hours in the boat-shed.

He gained the door and was endeavouring to get on to his feet, when he heard a faint sound from behind him. He held his breath and listened intently. The sound came again, and this time he was able to identify its location — it came from the boat. He rolled over in that direction, and somehow or other he managed to hoist himself into a standing position and, placing his bound hands on the edge of the boat, he levered his body up and threw himself head-first over the side. For a moment or two he lay there half-stunned. Then he heard the sound again, a groan, which this time came from very close at hand. He turned his throbbing head in the direction from which it came, and saw a huddled form in the stern of the boat. He dragged himself nearer and saw that it was Uisdean. His hands and feet were bound, and his face was ghastly pale and streaked with blood. He called his name softly, and then as he got no answer, louder and more urgently. He fancied he saw a flicker of consciousness on his face, his eyelids fluttered for an instant, then he groaned and lay so still that Colin was paralysed with fear.

He lay flat on his stomach on the bottom of the boat and tried to conquer the dread that had taken possession

125

of him and inhibited action. Uisdean was dying, he was sure of that, if he did not act quickly it would be too late. Perhaps it was already too late, he thought desperately, looking at the white, blood-stained face and the motionless figure. If only he could get his hands free. Somewhere about the boat there must be a sharp edge on which he could rub the rope which bound his hands until it frayed, and he could burst the fetters. That was, he knew, from his adventure stories, how the hero escaped. But there was nothing that he could see that would suit his purpose. Then he remembered Uisdean's knife — there was just a chance that their assailant had not searched the pocket in the lining of his jacket, where Uisdean always carried it.

He dragged himself painfully over the planks. Feeling had returned to his arms and legs and now they felt as if red-hot needles were being stuck into them. He gritted his teeth and inched himself forward until he reached his friend, then felt for the knife. To his relief it was still there. He drew it out, and holding it in his bound hands, he managed to open the big blade with his teeth. Then gripping it between the palms of his hands, he sawed at the cord that bound his feet until it was frayed and, finally, with a jerk he sundered it. The next step was to free his hands, which he did by placing the knife between his knees and rubbing the rope against the blade.

He now turned his attention to Uisdean, cutting the cords that bound him and placing his jacket under his head. Next he soaked his handkerchief in the water that lay between the planks of the boat, and began to bathe his forehead, anxiously watching the pale face for a sign of life. When at last Uisdean stirred and opened his eyes, Colin was so relieved that he almost wept. To hide his emotion, he busied himself with washing away the blood from Uisdean's face and neck. By the time that little service was completed, he regained control over his features and voice.

"Ye had better lie still. Ah'm going to open that door like ah did the last time and go for help."

Uisdean tried to raise his head, but the effort made him feel so faint that he took Colin's advice and lay still.

"Ye're sure ye'll be all right? Ah won't be long," said Colin anxiously.

Uisdean managed a grin.

"Ah'm all right except that my head is like as if it was splitting in two halves. How about your own?"

"It's no' so bad."

"Ah think mine must be harder than yours!"

"Or Ross had maybe a little practice when he turned his attention to me!"

"It was Ross then? Ah didna have time to see his face before ah was knocked out."

"Aye, it was Ross all right. There was a couple of others with him, too. Do you know, Col, I would have got away if I had not caught my foot in a hole and come down. Then before I could get up, one of them was on top of me and then someone else was banging me on the head."

He felt his forehead and the back of his head.

"There is a fine-sized bump on it."

"Aye, ah know. Ah thought you were finished for good and all. You're quite sure that you will be all right, ah mean, you're no' going to pass out again or anything like that?"

"I will be up on my feet again in no time."

"That's fine, but don't move until ah come back. Ah'd better get a move on in case Ross comes back and gives us another dose."

"I do not think that that is very likely. It's my guess that

127

he and his accomplices are now miles away with their booty."

"Maybe I should have a look at the room behind the door to see whether they've cleared the stuff out."

"That can wait. You had better reserve your strength to get help. You are looking a bit the worse for wear, Col. Are you sure that you will manage?"

"Aye, ah'll manage," said Colin with forced confidence.

CHAPTER TWENTY-NINE

In reality he was anything but confident. His head was throbbing so badly that he could hardly see and he felt sick and dizzy. But not for anything would he have admitted it. This was his great moment — he was in charge of the situation and the fact that everything now depended on him outweighed the pain. He even waved his hand gaily to Uisdean as he climbed over the edge of the boat.

A few minutes later his head again appeared over the side.

"There's someone coming," he said. "Ah can hear voices. It could be Ross."

"Maybe it's a rescue party."

"Hardly," said Colin, "only Ross knows that we are here. It's more likely he's come back to get the goods."

Uisdean pulled himself painfully to his feet and stood swaying a little, holding onto the edge of the boat.

"I am thinking that we will have to be giving him a bittie of his own medicine," he said.

"Aye, but you stay where you are. Ah'll deal with this."

"Not on your life! I would not be missing it for anything."

Colin looked a little disappointed. Just for once he would have liked to win all the glory for himself. But Uisdean was once again taking charge. One by one, he threw the oars on to the floor and then climbed down himself. He was still deadly pale, but very composed.

"You will stand on one side of the door and I will take

the other. Then, when they come in we will let them have it with the oars. First blow to you," he added with a smile, realising even in the moment of crisis that Colin had wanted to have the credit for laying low their attackers.

They took up their stance on either side of the door and waited. Footsteps were approaching the shed and they heard the murmur of voices. Someone rattled the door and Colin had just time to think that that was curious. Then there was a loud thud, followed by another and another, until the door crashed open and a figure was catapulted into the room.

"Ah don't think," began Colin, but Uisdean's oar rose and fell.

There was a yelp of pain and an oath from the intruder. Uisdean drew back the oar again, preparing for the coup de grâce, when he felt it being seized and pulled out of his hand. He turned to defend himself, then fell back in amazement. A familiar figure stood behind him, a bulky figure in blue uniform, who was carefully propping the captured oar up against the wall. Uisdean stared at him, too amazed to utter a word. It was the policeman whom they called Roller. He looked at the first figure who had landed in a heap beside the boat, and who was now picking himself up — there was something familiar about him too, he thought, trying to place him with a mind that was still confused. The figure turned and faced them, one hand rubbing his shoulder where Uisdean's oar had caught him, his head nodding gently in their direction.

"It is a good thing," Noddy was saying, "that your aim is not very accurate."

Uisdean, still bewildered at the turn of events, began to stammer an apology, but Noddy interrupted him.

"I accept that the blow was not intended for me, so we

130

will not pursue the matter. There are other more urgent things to be attended to." Then turning to Roller, he went on,

"If it is all right with you, constable, I think I will be taking those young delinquents into custody before they do any more damage. And talking about damage, we had better see how much has been done to them."

"We're all right, sir," put in Colin quickly, "it's Ross we have to worry about."

Then assuming an air of great dignity, he turned to Roller.

"I can show you where they had their cache."

"Can you though?" said Roller, winking at Noddy. "We will have to be enlisting you in the force as soon as you are old enough."

"It"s the truth I'm telling you," said Colin indignantly, for he had noticed the wink. "Just follow me, constable."

He opened the door that led to the store-room and the passage. As Uisdean had surmised, the stuff was gone. Though he had expected it, Colin was a little disappointed, but he soon recovered.

"The passage," he pointed out importantly, "leads to the ruins of the old castle. That will be how they got the stuff out."

Roller looked suitably impressed.

"Is that so now?" he said. "Well, that would explain it."

"Explain what?"

"We were expecting to intercept them on the main road. So that is how they gave us the slip."

"Maybe you'd still catch them at the other end of the tunnel. Ah mean, there's just a chance, isn't there?"

"Don't worry. We'll get them all right."

"Would you like me to come with you? Ah could show you the exact place."

"No, my boy. You'd better go with your headmaster."

And though he pleaded with Roller and Noddy to be allowed to help in the capture of Ross and his associates, they were both adamant.

"But," said Roller, "your help has been invaluable. The only thing that I would find fault with is that you ought to have come to us sooner."

"You would only have laughed at us when we had no proof. We had to get the evidence and we had it, too, and we were coming with it to you when we were ambushed."

"We can discuss all that later," said Noddy, a little impatiently. "What is important now is to see that these boys have come to no harm. Besides, the constable here has work to do. Colin seems to be able to walk, but perhaps you could give me a hand with Uisdean, constable."

So, much against their will, the boys had to abandon any idea of being in at the kill. By the time they reached the headmaster's house, however, they were so exhausted that they made little protest when they were sent to bed.

Later, when the doctor called, he advised complete rest for twenty-four hours since Uisdean, at least, was suffering from slight concussion. Noddy himself brought them some breakfast and then left them, with strict instructions that there was to be no talking and that they were on no account to get up until he gave them permission. Then nodding benevolently, he left them and in a few minutes they were fast asleep.

CHAPTER THIRTY

Hours later Colin awoke. He had just time to wonder where he was and why the room was in darkness, when the door opened, a light was switched on and the headmaster came in, with a tray which he laid on the table beside the bed. Then he drew up a chair, sat down and said,

"Since Uisdean is still asleep, we will just leave him. But you had better eat this up and then you can get off to sleep again."

"Ah don't need any more sleep, sir. Ah've slept right round the clock. Ah'd rather get up and find out what's been happening."

"No doubt, no doubt. But you will just stay where you are until morning. I have informed your parents, so there is nothing for you to worry about. Eat up now and don't talk. Tomorrow morning you can do as much talking as you like, but tonight you will rest."

Colin obeyed and began to eat, while the headmaster watched him, nodding his head encouragingly each time that Colin looked up and met his eyes.

"Fine," he said, when the meal had been disposed of. "You look a lot better than you did this morning. Another night's rest and you will be completely recovered." He turned at the door with his hand on the light switch, and said,

"There is just one thing though that will perhaps make you sleep better — they have caught Ross. Goodnight to you now and sleep well."

133

Before Colin had time to ask any questions, Noddy had gone and the room was in darkness. He lay listening to the sound of Noddy's footsteps on the stairs and along the passage. Then a door opened and closed, and there was silence. But the news that the headmaster had so casually imparted was far from having the intended effect. All kinds of speculations about the method and place of the capture occupied his mind, so that he stared for a long time wide awake into the darkness.

A wind was beginning to rise, coming mysteriously from nowhere, so soft at first that it only stirred the curtains; then becoming bolder, it tugged at the window sashes, finally increasing in violence, it threw itself savagely against the house as if it would tear it to pieces. At intervals, when the wind had retreated to gather force for a still more violent onslaught, he could hear the waves dashing against the shore. Warm and comfortable in his bed, he thought about the cairn and whether the waves were high enough to cover it, and about the night he had been marooned on it, and how Ross had rescued him. He felt a twinge of remorse then for his part in bringing about his capture. The feeling was only momentary and was succeeded by one of pride in their achievement, and especially in the final stage of their adventure, when he had assumed command. Thus it was with a pleasant glow of satisfaction that he drifted off to sleep.

When next Colin awoke, the storm had abated. The house was very quiet and the sound of the waves was a murmur in the distance. He lay for a while listening to Uisdean's even breathing and the cries of the seagulls over the firth. It was not yet quite daylight, but he was so

134

wide-awake and rested that it irked him to have to stay in bed. For a moment he considered the idea of slipping out of the house and going down to the beach, but since his shoes had been taken away to be dried, that was impossible.

Presently he crept out of bed and prowled around the room in search of something to pass the time. But there was nothing, not even a book or magazine to interest him. He sat by the window watching the sky growing bright to the east beyond the hills on the far side of the firth and the water indolently lapping the shore.

As the light grew, he could just distinguish on a rock a little way out a grey heron, hunched in its self-sufficiency gazing at the sea. Still, completely self-contained and regardless of the gulls that wheeled and screamed over its head, it looked as if it had stood there from the beginning of time and would stand unmoved and unmoving to all eternity.

On the beach the oyster-catchers began to stir. Soon they were hunting assiduously, strutting self-importantly over the shingle as if nothing in the world mattered but their searching and scratching. Close to the shore a flock of ducks rocked gently on the waves. The family of swans awoke, and lazily uncoiling their necks began to up-end. Then above the skirling of the gulls, he heard another note, the lost call of the curlews, and presently they came into sight, flying low over the water, then wheeling in shorewards. He watched them alight and begin to rake among the seaweed with their long, sharp bills.

The sky was now flushed with red. Soon the sun rose from behind the hills and threw a band of gold over the water, tapering to the near shore. Coming from inland and flying into the sun, a flock of lapwings darted into view and began to perform their patterns. They soared and swooped in perfect order, flashing now black, now white, as if the colours were switched on and off at a word of command. He watched fascinated as they went through the same drill several times — black down to within an inch or two of the waves, veer and soar white, swoop again black — and never once did he catch a single one of the two score or more out of pattern.

A sound from the room diverted his attention from the shore. Uisdean had turned over and his quilt had slipped to the floor. Colin went to pick it up and replace it on the bed. As he bent over him, Uisdean opened his eyes, looked blankly at his friend for a moment, then said,

"How long have I been sleeping. You might have wakened me."

"Ah didn't dare. Ah had strict orders not to disturb you on any account. Ye've slept two whole rounds of the clock, you sluggard!"

"It will have been the pills, I expect."

"Is your head better?'

"It is just fine, except for this bump. What time would it be, do you think?"

"Ah don't know. About seven ah would say, since the sun's just up over the horizon."

"I wish it was breakfast time — I am starving. When do you suppose Noddy has breakfast?"

"Not for hours. He's always late — half past eight, ah should say, at the earliest."

"An hour and a half, and I am so ravenous I could eat an ox!"

"Ah could sneak downstairs and see if there is any food around. Wait a minute, though — what about the biscuits and chocolate we brought last night. We didn't eat any of it. It must still be in your coat. Ah saw it hanging in the lobby last night. Ah'll see if it's still there."

136

"Mind that you do not wake up Noddy."

"Ah'll be as stealthy as a wolf."

★   ★   ★   ★

"That is the best breakfast I have ever had," said Uisdean, chewing appreciatively at the last biscuit. "And to think that if Ross had not slugged us, we would have eaten them already. It is an ill-wind —"

"By the way, Ross has been caught. Noddy told me last night."

"And it is only now that you are telling me! Did he say where?"

"No, he went off before ah could ask any questions. He is a nuisance — ah'm dying to know what happened."

"What is puzzling me is how Noddy and Roller knew where to find us."

"Maybe the police were on to him all the time; ah mean, keeping an eye on him and just waiting to catch him in the act."

"Hmm. It could be. I cannot think of any other explanation."

"In which case they'd have caught him anyway, and all our sleuthing was for nothing."

"Don't look so downcast, Col. After all, we did have a lot of fun."

"Ah was hoping they'd give us a reward or a medal or something. But if they knew all the time maybe we will only be getting into trouble for not telling them about it sooner."

"They did not know about Ross's store and about the passage until we told them."

"Aye, that's true. So maybe after all —"

"Just wait and we will soon be seeing," said Uisdean.

CHAPTER THIRTY-ONE

When they questioned Noddy at breakfast, he either could not or would not give them any information. In fact, he was not inclined to converse with them at all. Breakfast, he informed them, was a time when he liked a little peace and quiet. Apart from that remark, all that they could get out of him was that they were not to go to school that morning, since the police would be coming to see them and they would have to make a statement. For a while, the two boys were silent digesting this information. Colin especially was very pleased. It was proof to him that their efforts had not been in vain and as he ate he rehearsed to himself what he would say. He was still clothing the events in a suitably dramatic form when Noddy, who had been waiting for the boys to finish, rose from the table, telling them that he had some things to see to before the arrival of the police, and that they could go out into the garden when they had finished breakfast.

"Couldn't we go down to the beach?" said Colin eagerly. "Ah mean, there may be some clues there, especially at the place where he slugged us."

But Noddy vetoed the idea. On no account, he said, were they to leave the garden. Then he added drily that they appeared to have completely forgotten that the beach was out of bounds to them. He might have said a good deal more, if Uisdean had not at that moment created a diversion. He had been standing by the window looking out at the shore, when he saw three figures coming into view.

"I think that that is the police now, sir," he said.

Colin rushed to the window and was in time to catch a glimpse of them before they turned in from the road to the drive.

"It's them all right! Anyway, it is Roller, ah mean, Constable Grant and someone in plain clothes, and ah don't know about the third — he looked very small, almost like a boy."

Noddy smiled and said cryptically,

"It could be."

In a few moments, they saw the three figures coming into sight round the bend of the drive. As he had said, it was Roller, quite unmistakeable from his gait, and a tall man they did not know, and the third was quite certainly a boy. Colin stared at him in amazement, then rubbed his eyes and pressed his face close up to the window to have a better view. Uisdean at his side glanced at his friend, his eyes round with astonishment.

"Will you be looking at that now? It is Hugh himself, as large as life, that is with them!"

Still unable to believe their eyes, the two boys gazed at the approaching group. If they had not been so dumbfounded, they would have found something comical in the sight of fat, little Hugh trotting along between the two, tall policemen. He was having difficulty in keeping up with them and when he fell behind, he would give a little hop and skip to catch up with them. They could see that he was feeling the importance of his position from the earnest way he kept looking now at one, now at the other. It was apparent, too, that the two men were treating him as if he were an equal, for they could see them

139

inclining their heads towards him and listening with interest to what he had to say.

Uisdean turned to the headmaster, who was nodding gently in the direction of the group who were now passing the window.

"Whatever is Hugh doing with them?" he asked.

"You will hear all about that in a moment," said Noddy, who appeared to be secretly amused at the boys' amazement.

He went to open the door and the boys heard him greeting his visitors. Next moment he was ushering them into the room and bringing in two chairs for them. Roller and the tall man, whom Noddy introduced as Superintendent Mearns, seated themselves at a table and brought out some papers, which they spread out before them.

Meanwhile Hugh went over to his schoolmates with a broad smile of greeting, evidently sure that they would welcome him with equal cordiality. Even the brief nod of acknowledgement he received from them did not appear to affect his good-humour.

Yet in spite of their curt greeting, the boys were not a little impressed by his demeanour. Here was a new Hugh, self-possessed, and in spite of his absurd little legs and large head, there was a dignity about him which they did not fail to note. Still with a quiet smile on his face, he went and sat down in one of the chairs which Noddy had pulled up. Superintendent Mearns indicated, with a wave of his hand, that Uisdean and Colin were to take the vacant seats on the other side of the table beside Hugh. There was now silence in the room, except for the rustling of the papers which the Superintendent read through before turning his attention to the waiting boys.

"I have here," he began at last, "a statement made by

140

Hugh Rennie. I would now like to hear the whole story from you, too. Take your time about it. Constable Grant here will take it down. Who is to be the spokesman?"

"Ah will," said Colin quickly. Then he added, turning to Uisdean, "That is, if you don't mind? Ah prepared it in my mind when you were asleep."

The Superintendent nodded approvingly.

"Good. Begin right at the beginning and don't leave anything out."

Colin was in his element. He thoroughly enjoyed being in the centre of the stage, and related the story from beginning to end with great fluency, pausing only occasionally to turn to Uisdean to corroborate a detail. When he had finished, the Superintendent congratulated him and asked a few questions. Then Uisdean and Colin signed their statement and the formal part of the proceedings was over.

"You know, I suppose," said the Superintendent, "that Ross has been captured. We got him and his associates as they were transporting the stuff from the tunnel to a lorry. But for you two, we would not have known about the tunnel. No doubt, we'd have caught them in the end. We set up road-blocks and took all the usual measures, but because of your information, we got them a great deal sooner and with less trouble. For that I want to thank you and it may be that later our thanks will assume a more concrete form. But," and here he looked severely at Uisdean and Colin, "I am bound to say that you handled this badly at one point. Perhaps you realise yourselves what the mistake was?"

"You mean we should have come to you at once," said Colin. "But you see, we wanted to have proof."

"When you found the stuff in the tunnel, that was proof enough, wasn't it?"

141

"Aye, a suppose so."

"The truth is that you wanted to tie it all up yourselves."

The boys nodded.

"It was your adventure and you were determined to see it through to the end. And because of your recklessness, you almost got yourselves killed. But for Hugh here, who showed great commonsense in realising that he could not tackle the thing himself and came to us at once, goodness knows what might have happened to you."

"Ah could have got out," said Colin, who was vexed at the lecture and thought it unjust that Hugh should be singled out for such unqualified praise. "Ah was just about to come for help, when Roll— when Mr Grant and Mr Munro burst the door open."

"I should think you were hardly in a state to go for help at that moment."

Then, as Colin was about to argue the point, he held up his hand to silence him and went on,

"I do want to stress this point very emphatically. The correct procedure would have been to go to the police at the very latest when you discovered the smuggled goods. Is that understood?"

Rather crestfallen, the two boys nodded. Seeing their discomfiture, the Superintendent smiled at them.

"Fine! We'll say no more about that. Taking everything into consideration and making due allowance for an excess of enthusiasm on your part, you did a very good job. Ross and his friends were dangerous. The stuff was, as you discovered, dumped for them on the cairn by their accomplices. We suspect that it came from Norwegian ships, but we are following this up. The most sinister aspect of their activities was that they were importing large quantities of drugs into the country."

142

"The white powder in the boxes?"

"Yes, that's right. We've been trying to find out for a long time where the supplies were coming from. Now we know and this particular source will be eliminated. So you see, you have done a really valuable public service. And now, since I have a train to catch, I shall regretfully have to cut our acquaintance short. Who knows? — we may meet again."

When Roller and the Superintendent were gone, Noddy added his strictures on their handling of the affair, so that there should be no doubt left in their minds of the correct course to take should they ever again be involved in a similar situation. Nor did he forget to admonish them for their disobedience in going on to the beach. The lecture, however, was the only punishment he imposed on them, and once he had delivered it, he unbent and said that apart from these points, he was pleased with their conduct. Hugh, of course, he exempted from all blame, in fact, once more he came in for special commendation. You would imagine, Colin thought bitterly, that it was he who had unmasked Ross instead of taking advantage of all their spade work and then running to the police.

CHAPTER THIRTY-TWO

"There isna any sign of a struggle at all," said Colin in disgust. "You'd think that there'd be at least something to mark the spot, but there isna even a footprint."

"There would hardly be any on the grass," said Hugh reasonably.

Taking no notice of the remark, Colin pursued,

"Nor a drop o' blood."

The three boys had been excused school for the rest of the morning, and as a special concession, had been allowed to go down to the beach to re-visit the scene of their adventure.

"We could maybe be putting up a little cairn, Col," said Uisdean, "to mark the place of our epic struggle."

"You did not have time to struggle," observed Hugh. "He jumped on you from behind that bush there, and then — whang — whang — you were both out cold before you had time to do anything."

"Ah know that. You don't have to tell us."

"You must have been pretty close then," said Uisdean, "when you saw all that."

"Aye, and why didn't you warn us, since you're so smart?" said Colin.

"I wanted to, of course, but put yourself in my place — it was a very tricky situation. I had to think quickly and make a decision. I could either warn you and so draw attention to myself, in which case they'd have got all three of us, or to lie low — I was crouching in the bushes a few yards away from them — and escape to raise the alarm."

"If you'd shouted a warning, we could have got away from him. Ah bet you anything you like ah — we — can run faster than them."

"Perhaps you are right," said Hugh, in even tones, "it is difficult to know in an emergency what is the right thing to do. Maybe, too, I acted instinctively without really thinking about it."

"Perhaps you acted to save your own skin," said Colin.

"I do not think that is a fair remark," said Uisdean. "It would not have helped anyone if Hugh had got himself knocked over the head too. In the circumstances, I would say that he made the right decision."

"Well, ah·don't agree," said Colin.

Although in his heart he knew that Uisdean was right, he was too stubborn to admit it. Uisdean went on as if he had not heard his objection.

"And then you would have waited in your hiding-place until Ross had disposed of us, I suppose?"

"Yes. Or at least, until they took Colin. As soon as they were out of sight, I came out. You were lying there unconscious, Uisdean. I did not like leaving you; I did try to bring you round, but it was no use, and then I didn't dare wait too long in case they got me when they came back for you. It wasn't easy, I hated having to go. It seemed so awful deserting you — and I — well, you do believe me, don't you, that I didn't want to? Only I thought —"

"Yes, I do believe you, Hugh. It was a tricky situation to be in, but I would have done the same myself if I had been in your shoes."

Hugh went on, knowing that Colin was still sceptical, and feeling the need to justify himself in his eyes, too.

"I couldn't carry you, you see. I did try, but I couldn't

even move you. I thought that if I could drag you even as far as the road, there might be a chance that someone would come along. But as I say, you were a dead weight and I could not even budge you a yard, so I gave it up and ran as fast as I could, and then my wretched asthma started, so that kept me for some time. It was awful knowing that time was so precious and not being able to do anything till it passed off."

"Poor Hugh, I can imagine how it must have been."

"Well, then, when I could go on again —"

"You went to the police station."

"Well, I was on my way there when I ran slap into Roller, who was on his rounds. He was so slow on the uptake, it took me ages to make him understand. I think he thought I was up to something. Anyway, at last he took me to the station and got on to his H.Q. and they seemed to talk some sense into him, for he changed his tune after that. I wanted to come back with him and rescue you, but nothing doing. He roused Noddy from his bed and they set out to look for you. They took me back to the hostel; I hardly slept a wink wondering what was happening. And then Noddy sent for me yesterday and told me they'd found you and that you were all right, and that Ross had been caught. And this morning Roller and the Superintendent came for me and brought me here. Well, that's about all, I think."

"There is just one other thing that is not quite clear to me," said Uisdean. "I suppose that you saw us leave the dormitory and that you followed us down to the beach?"

"Yes, I pretended to be asleep. You see, I suspected all along that you were up to something."

"So you trailed us to the shore then, and you stayed there all the time we were out on the cairn?"

"Yes. You were already quite a long way out when I

146

reached the beach, and I'd been going pretty hard to try to catch up with you, so I was feeling pretty rotten even then, so I thought I'd better not attempt the mud flats."

"More likely you were scared," said Colin scornfully, but once more neither of the others paid any attention to him.

Feeling humiliated and aggrieved, Colin left them and walked towards the edge of the water. He was hoping that Uisdean would follow him, but the two boys did not even seem to notice that he had gone. Feeling very miserable and lonely, he stared out at the Black Cairn, whose hump he could see rising above the waves. He was out of it again, without a friend in the world, just as he used to be when Allan and his friends ran away from him. All the old feelings of inadequacy and wretchedness came over him and he wished that they had never stumbled on Ross's secret, since it had only brought Hugh and Uisdean together and left him, as always, the odd man out.

He glanced back to where the two were standing. They were talking and laughing as if they were already life-long friends. It was obvious to him that they had completely forgotten him. For all they cared he might not even exist. No-one was bothering about him, no-one in the whole world. He began to walk away from them towards the boat-house, his shoulders hunched and his hands thrust deep into his pockets, brooding over his wrongs. He would show them that he did not care, that he did not want their friendship. He did not need anyone, he'd stand alone as he had done before. He began to run, tearing wildly along the beach, running away from them, running away from the misery that, in spite of his attempts at self-sufficiency, he could not throw off. When he'd exhausted himself he threw himself down on the shore and stared out over the firth.

147

The grey heron was standing motionless, hunched on his rock intently watching the water and oblivious of his surroundings. Some yards away to his left, some redshanks were scratching busily among the seaweed, and a little colony of goosanders were rocking about on the waves. A company of cormorants, with stiff, intent necks, swept over the water in formation. On the cairn, a black-backed gull was perched, the restless oyster-catchers were raking the foreshore and a few dunlins ran after the waves as they receded.

The sight of so many birds restored his spirits a little. He pictured himself lonely and heroic, as indifferent to everyone and as dignified in his solitude as the grey heron. This image of himself pleased him so much that he began to feel magnanimous towards Uisdean. He would forgive him for his desertion, though he would never be his close friend again, even though he came and begged him. As for Hugh, he was no longer angry with him, he was so poor a figure that he was not worth bothering about. The best way to treat him was with cool disdain.

But somehow, build it up as he would, the picture was not wholly satisfactory. Something was disturbing it, a little nagging doubt at the back of his mind that he had not behaved well that morning. Quite soon, for changes in mood with Colin were swift, the little doubt became a certainty. It was he who was at fault, not Uisdean. Uisdean, as usual, had been right and he had been wrong, and ungrateful to gibe at Hugh. He looked towards them; they were still deep in conversation, still apparently unaware that he had gone. He knew what he ought to do, but he was still not ready for it. The struggle between conscience and pride continued, and he stared gloomily out at the firth trying to sort out the confusion of his feelings.

All at once, he heard a shout and turned his head. So they had not completely forgotten him, he thought with satisfaction. But he did not move yet, for he was not quite ready to be reconciled. A second shout and a wave from Uisdean brought him to his feet. He stood hesitantly, looking in their direction. Then he saw Uisdean break into his long, loping stride and that was the gesture he had been waiting for. He, too, began to run and with every step he took towards them, the weight on his mind lightened. Hugh he could see was trotting behind Uisdean, doing his best to keep up with him. As he ran he came to a decision. The lonely, heroic figure had completely faded from his mind. He was very ashamed of himself now, but equally determined to do the one thing that could restore his self-esteem. So when he came up with them, he looked straight at Hugh, and taking a deep breath, said,

"Ah'm sorry, Hugh. Ah was wrong just now — you did a very good job."

Hugh's heavy face lit up with a quick flash of pleasure and Uisdean smiled at Colin, and said,

"Pretty good team work, I am thinking."

Colin grinned back. "If we'd known he was going to be such a good sleuth, we'd have included him in the ploy, wouldn't we, Uisdean?"

"Yes, we would at that. In the future, we will have to be thinking about making use of his talents."

Hugh was speechless with delight, but still sufficiently in command of himself to feel that such a great occasion demanded some formal gesture of recognition. Drawing his stout, little figure to its full height, he stood at attention and saluted.

"Always at your service," he said.

Then suddenly, while they were still laughing at Hugh's

idea of marking the event, he stood on his head, bounced up again and turned a cartwheel. Soon they were all vying with one another in handstands and cartwheels, until Colin called a halt.

"Ye'd better no' overdo it, Hugh," he said.

So they sat for a while talking and watching the flight of the birds over the firth. Then with Hugh trotting happily between them, they walked back along the beach.